The Mind's Verdict

Copyright Page

The Minds of Justice Series: Book 1

Title: *The Mind's Verdict*
Author: Jerome Wright

Copyright © [2024] by Jerome Wright
All rights reserved.

No part of this publication may be reproduced, distributed, or transmitted in any form or by any means, including photocopying, recording, or other electronic or mechanical methods, without the prior written permission of the publisher, except in the case of brief quotations embodied in critical reviews and certain other non-commercial uses permitted by copyright law. For permission requests, please contact the publisher.

This is a work of fiction. Names, characters, places, and incidents are either the products of the author's imagination or used fictitiously. Any resemblance to actual persons, living or dead, or actual events is purely coincidental.

Table of Contents

Chapter 1. The Arrest---8

Chapter 2. Building the case---11

Chapter 3. Shadows of the past---17

Chapter 4. The first court appearance---22

Chapter 5. Uncovering secrets---27

Chapter 6. The first thread---33

Chapter 7. A revelation from the past---39

Chapter 8. Pressure mounts---45

Chapter 9. The memory trap---51

Chapter 10. The similar case---56

Chapter 11. The trial preparations---62

Chapter 12. The first day in court---67

Chapter 13. An unseen manipulator---72

Chapter 14. Expert testimonies---78

Chapter 15. A desperate discovery---84

Chapter 16. Closer to the truth---90

Chapter 17. The shocking confession---96

Chapter 18. The final argument---102

Chapter 19. Verdict and aftermath---107

Chapter 20. Reflections and shadows---112

Preface

The Mind's Verdict explores the fragile intersections of mental health, justice, and the human psyche. This novel is born from an interest in the grey areas of the law, those spaces where questions of morality and accountability blur the boundaries of guilt and innocence. At its heart, it is a story of resilience, trauma, and the human desire to be understood—even when facing society's harshest judgment.

In writing The Mind's Verdict, I wanted to create a story that would challenge readers to look beyond the facts of a case and consider the often-unseen complexities that shape people's lives. The characters in this novel—Rachel, Eli, and Emily—each grapple with their own limitations and perceptions, each bringing a unique perspective to the unfolding drama. As they navigate the high-stakes world of a courtroom trial, they're forced to confront deep-seated truths about themselves, their beliefs, and their roles within the justice system.

This book is the first in The Minds of Justice series, a collection that will continue to delve into the intersections of law and psychology, asking difficult questions about accountability, empathy, and the human condition. I invite you, the reader, to journey with these characters, to step into the shoes of those who fight for justice—even when justice itself feels elusive.

Thank you for reading, and welcome to The Minds of Justice.

Jerome Wright

Acknowledgements

Writing *The Mind's Verdict* has been a journey made possible through the unwavering support, encouragement, and inspiration of many incredible people.

To my family, thank you for believing in my passion for storytelling and for reminding me to keep going, even on the toughest days. Your love and support are the foundation upon which all my work is built.

A heartfelt thank you to my friends and colleagues who inspired and encouraged me throughout the writing process. Your insightful conversations and genuine feedback helped shape this story into what it is today.

To my editor, thank you for your keen eye and invaluable guidance, which brought this story to life in ways I hadn't imagined. Your dedication to every detail and your commitment to this project have been a gift.

To my readers, both new and returning, thank you for embarking on this journey with me. Your enthusiasm for my work drives my creativity and reminds me of the incredible power of storytelling. I am grateful for your trust and your willingness to explore the questions and mysteries that lie in the grey areas of justice and humanity.

Finally, this book wouldn't be complete without acknowledging all the legal and mental health professionals who work tirelessly to seek justice and support those navigating the complexities of mental health. Their commitment to truth, compassion, and understanding inspired this novel's themes and reminded me of the importance of empathy in all things.

With gratitude,

Jerome Wright

Chapter 1: The Arrest

Rachel Yates' phone buzzed, vibrating off the wooden nightstand like it was trying to escape. She squinted at the glowing screen, her vision blurred from a restless half-sleep. 3:17 a.m. An unknown number—another call to her private line, the one she didn't list on any business card or website.

She answered, forcing her voice into a register of alertness. "This is Rachel Yates."

There was a muffled sound, a slight hiccup of breath on the other end. "Is... is this the lawyer?" The voice was female, soft and breaking, like she was barely holding back something jagged.

Rachel sat up, her instincts kicking in. "Who's calling?"

The woman's breaths grew rapid. "I... I didn't mean to. I didn't mean for any of it to happen," she whispered, her words scattering like leaves in the wind.

Rachel's hand tightened around the phone. "Who is this?"

"Emily. Emily Grant," she said, her voice trembling as she spoke her name, as if she wasn't quite sure it belonged to her.

Rachel's mind raced, trying to place the name. Then it clicked—Emily Grant, the young woman her partner had mentioned in passing, a client seeking legal representation for a domestic dispute. A bruised wife with an unfinished story, he had said.

"Emily, are you safe?" Rachel asked, carefully lowering her voice.

There was a hollow pause. "I… I don't know."

Rachel's pulse quickened. "Where are you?"

"I think… the police station. They say I… they think I killed him." Emily's words landed like stones, each one heavier than the last.

Rachel swung her legs over the side of the bed, her heart pounding against her ribs. "Stay calm, Emily. I'm on my way."

The fluorescent lights of the precinct felt almost aggressive, casting sharp lines and deep shadows that stretched across the linoleum floor. Rachel strode in, heels clicking with the sharp authority she'd perfected over years of courtroom battles. She flashed her ID to the tired-looking officer behind the desk.

"I'm here for Emily Grant."

The officer raised an eyebrow, sizing her up before he gestured toward the holding area. "Good luck with that one," he muttered. "She's been staring at the wall for an hour. Doesn't even blink."

Rachel ignored the comment, her attention already focused on the figure hunched in the corner of the holding cell. Emily Grant sat alone; her slender frame dwarfed by the harsh iron bars. Her dark hair fell limply around her face, and her eyes stared blankly at something only she could see.

Rachel approached; her heels muffled by the thick concrete floor. She crouched down to meet Emily's eye level, a whisper of compassion breaking through her professional veneer.

"Emily?" she said softly, wrapping her voice in a gentleness she usually reserved for her rarest clients—the ones for whom the word "guilty" didn't fit so easily.

Emily's gaze shifted, almost as if she were waking from a dream. Her eyes met Rachel's, and they were glassy, hollow. Rachel felt a shiver prick her spine. She knew that look. It was the look of someone standing on the thin edge of reality, about to slip through.

"I… I didn't…" Emily's voice was thin, barely more than a breath. She pressed her hands against her temples, as if trying to steady herself. "I didn't mean to… to hurt him. I just… I don't remember."

Rachel inhaled, steadying herself. This wasn't the typical first meeting. "Emily, listen to me. You don't have to say anything right now. But I need you to tell me exactly what you remember."

Emily closed her eyes, trembling as she pulled in a shuddering breath. "I remember… going home. His face, he was… angry. So angry. And then… I remember the knife… in my hand." She choked on the words, clutching her arms around herself. "But I didn't mean to."

Rachel's throat tightened, a flicker of dread sparking inside her. Her instincts were rarely wrong. This was no ordinary case.

Chapter 2: Building the Case

Rachel Yates sat in her office, staring at the message she'd typed out to Dr. Eli Warren.

I need your help with a new case. It's... complicated.

The word seemed woefully insufficient, yet Rachel couldn't think of anything better. Complicated didn't begin to cover the mess Emily Grant had found herself in—or the tangle that Rachel herself was now part of. A young woman with blood on her hands, eyes full of fear, and a memory too clouded to make sense of. If anyone could help her unravel the truth, it was Eli.

She pressed "Send" and waited, her mind spiralling through the possibilities. Eli Warren was one of the best forensic psychologists in the country, with a knack for diving into the darkest corners of the mind. They'd worked together years ago on a similarly twisted case, and she respected his insight and cautious objectivity. She respected him so much, in fact, that she knew he'd be sceptical from the start.

Her phone chimed with a response.

Meet me at the usual place in an hour. This better be worth it.

An hour later, Rachel slid into a leather booth at a quiet downtown café, the kind of place that had survived only because its customers valued discretion over ambience. Eli was already there, his fingers tapping out a restless rhythm on his coffee cup. He glanced up as she approached, his eyes narrowing in that intense, assessing way she remembered so well.

"Rachel," he said, folding his hands. "Complicated, you said?"

She nodded, slipping off her coat and taking the seat across from him. "More than complicated. The client is a young woman, Emily Grant. Mid-twenties, married, no prior record, no history of violence, at least as far as I can tell."

He raised an eyebrow. "And yet she's sitting in a holding cell for murder."

"Yes." Rachel paused, unsure of where to begin. She had replayed her conversation with Emily a dozen times since last night, searching for any clear answer—and finding none. "Her husband was found dead, and she was standing over him when the police arrived. Blood on her hands, knife on the floor."

Eli nodded slowly, but his expression remained neutral, almost detached. "Rachel, a lot of defendants claim they 'don't remember' committing a crime. Are you saying she has a documented dissociative disorder?"

"That's part of what I need you to help me figure out," she said, leaning forward. "Emily is different. There's something… fractured about her. When I spoke with her, she seemed genuinely lost. I'm not saying she's innocent, but if she did do this, I'm not convinced she was fully conscious of it. At least, not in a conventional sense."

"Dissociation?" he asked, his voice edged with a hint of scepticism.

"Yes," she said, nodding. "From what I observed, she seems to slip in and out of these… alternate states. One moment, she's Emily, and the next, she's someone else—someone who holds an entirely different set of memories."

He considered this, his gaze sharpening with interest. "So, you're suggesting she may have dissociative identity disorder?"

Rachel hesitated. "I'm not jumping to that conclusion. But there's something deeply unsettling about her mental state, and the more I look into her background, the more I see patterns of trauma that could support it."

Eli took a sip of his coffee, his eyes never leaving her. "The courts are notoriously sceptical of DID as a defence. It's one of the most controversial diagnoses out there. Many psychologists don't even believe it's real—or if it is, that it could lead someone to kill."

"I know," Rachel replied. "But if there's any chance her mental state could mitigate her responsibility—if she was manipulated, even unconsciously—I need to pursue it."

Eli sighed, leaning back. "I'll admit, I'm curious. But a jury isn't going to be as receptive to theories. They want clear facts, especially in a murder trial. And when you're dealing with trauma, memory gaps, dissociative states… it gets messy. Messy doesn't win cases, Rachel."

Rachel leaned forward; her gaze unwavering. "That's why I need you. You know how to explain these things, to make them real, to cut through the scepticism. Emily deserves someone who will give her the benefit of the doubt—someone who will at least try to understand what's happening in her mind."

For a moment, silence stretched between them, punctuated only by the quiet hum of the café. Eli studied her, his expression softening as he considered her plea. He'd been pulled into cases like this before, where the truth lay hidden beneath layers of trauma and tangled memories. He knew how ugly it could get—how haunting.

"Alright," he finally said, nodding. "I'll meet with her. But, Rachel…" His voice turned serious. "You need to be prepared for what we might uncover. If she's truly dissociative, there's a chance she doesn't just have a memory problem. There could be parts of her mind that even she doesn't understand."

Rachel arranged for Eli to meet Emily at the detention centre the following morning. She was both relieved and uneasy as they sat in the small, sterile interview room, waiting for Emily to arrive. The walls were white and featureless, the air heavy with the faint odour of antiseptic and stale coffee.

Eli glanced at Rachel. "Do you think she's stable enough to handle an evaluation like this?"

"She needs us to try," Rachel replied. "Emily might not be able to fully articulate what's going on inside her, but I think there's a part of her that desperately wants to be understood."

The door opened, and Emily was led in, her wrists in handcuffs, her face pale and expressionless. She seemed smaller than Rachel remembered, almost fragile, as though the weight of her reality had physically diminished her.

Eli observed her with a clinical curiosity, his gaze tracking her movements as she sat down across from them. He offered her a gentle smile; one Rachel had seen him use on countless clients before. It was a smile meant to reassure, to disarm.

"Emily, I'm Dr. Eli Warren," he said, his voice calm and measured. "Rachel's asked me to speak with you, just to understand a bit more about what you're experiencing."

Emily looked down, her fingers nervously twisting in her lap. "I don't… I don't know how much help I can be," she murmured. "Sometimes, I feel like I'm not even… here."

Eli nodded. "That's alright. Just start with what you remember, if that's okay with you."

She swallowed, her gaze fixed on her hands. "I remember… being angry, I think. My husband and I were arguing. He was yelling, and I felt… like I was fading. And then everything just… stopped. When I came to, he was on the floor, and there was blood, and I…" Her voice broke, and she looked away, eyes glistening.

Eli exchanged a glance with Rachel, his expression shifting from curiosity to something deeper. He leaned forward slightly, speaking softly. "Emily, have you ever had moments like this before? Moments where you felt… disconnected from yourself?"

She nodded slowly, looking up at him with a haunted expression. "It's been happening for as long as I can remember. Sometimes I wake up and there are whole days I can't recall. It's like… pieces of me just go missing."

Eli's gaze softened. "And do these pieces ever come back? Do you ever remember things later on?"

"Sometimes," she whispered. "But they don't feel like mine. They're like memories from a movie I've watched, not… my life."

Rachel felt a chill run through her. She knew dissociation could manifest in strange, unsettling ways, but hearing it from Emily—so raw, so fragmented—brought an unsettling weight to the reality of her experience. This wasn't just a defence. This was Emily's life, fractured and lost.

Eli leaned back, crossing his arms thoughtfully. "Emily, I'm going to be honest with you. We're exploring very difficult territory here. Your mind may be hiding things from you, things you're not ready to face. But if we're going to help you, I need you to trust us and be as open as you can."

Emily's gaze flickered to Rachel, as if seeking silent permission. Rachel nodded, offering a small smile of encouragement.

"I'll try," Emily whispered, her voice barely audible. She seemed on the edge of tears, but she held herself together, taking a shuddering breath.

Eli studied her for a long moment, and Rachel could see his resolve beginning to solidify. This wasn't just a case to him anymore; it was a chance to delve into the unknown, to seek answers in the darkest corners of a fractured mind.

As they wrapped up the session, Rachel's mind buzzed with possibilities and questions. The journey ahead was bound to be murky, fraught with scepticism and doubt. But one thing was clear: they had only begun to scratch the surface of what Emily's mind was hiding.

And Rachel knew, with a shiver of both fear and excitement, that Eli was now fully invested.

Chapter 3: Shadows of the Past

Rachel sat alone in her office, the yellowed file spread open on her desk, casting its secrets under the harsh glare of her reading lamp. She'd finally managed to get her hands on a detailed report from Child Protective Services. And what she saw in Emily's past was unsettling, enough to send a shiver through even the most hardened legal professional.

The file was thick, pages crammed with notes, evaluations, reports from teachers, and statements from neighbours. Each document painted a grim picture of Emily's upbringing, a pattern of trauma that read like a roadmap of brokenness and fractured memories.

She flipped through the pages, stopping at a report dated when Emily was just seven years old. The notes, written in a clinical hand, outlined an incident with stark, cold detachment:

"Subject Emily Grant found in a locked bathroom at home, unresponsive. Mother stated she 'lost control' during an argument with stepfather. Police called after neighbours reported hearing screams. Emily observed to be in a dissociative state upon arrival, exhibiting uncharacteristic behaviour and unresponsive to direct questions. No physical injuries noted, but mental evaluation recommended."

Rachel stared at the words, her mind racing to connect the dots. This was Emily's introduction to violence, to the emotional landscape that shaped her childhood—a landscape of fear and fractured trust. No wonder Emily's memory had splintered; her mind had been forced to build walls to protect her from the onslaught.

Rachel's eyes drifted to the next report, another incident only a year later. This time, Emily's mother was found unconscious, and Emily was crouched by her side, hands covered in blood—though it turned out to be from a broken vase. Witnesses had reported that Emily seemed to have "checked out," lost somewhere inside herself. And as Rachel read on, she sensed a disturbing pattern: each incident growing in intensity, each trauma carving deeper fractures into Emily's psyche.

Rachel leaned back in her chair, her fingers drumming on the desk as she absorbed the weight of Emily's history. The scenes played out in her mind like haunting snapshots from a life filled with violence and confusion. She could practically see Emily, a small child, curled up in terror, mind slipping away into safer, blank spaces.

The next report was even harder to read. It came from her high school counsellor, detailing a violent outburst during gym class. A classmate had said something that triggered Emily, and she'd lunged, her hands reaching for the girl's throat. It had taken two teachers to pull her away, and when they did, she didn't even remember what she'd done.

"Emily appears completely detached after the incident," the report read. *"When asked about her behaviour, she denies any memory of it. Displays signs consistent with trauma-induced dissociation."*

Rachel sighed, feeling the weight of it all. Emily wasn't just a woman struggling with a single traumatic event; she was a lifetime of wounds, layered over each other until they fused into something volatile, something dark. Each incident was like a scar, both healed and unhealed, bleeding just beneath the surface.

Rachel took a break, stepping out into the corridor. Her mind buzzed with questions, memories of Emily's broken gaze and trembling hands. She felt her heart twist, conflicted by a gnawing uncertainty. She believed in fighting for justice, but what if justice meant peeling back layers of Emily's trauma that were best left undisturbed? And worse yet—what if, by exploring Emily's mind, they uncovered a darker truth?

Returning to her office, she flipped back through the documents, looking for any details that might explain Emily's descent. Her fingers paused over a counsellor's note:

"Emily displays signs of repressed anger and dissociative behaviour, especially after physical abuse by stepfather. Care recommended but refused by mother. Emily may suffer from undiagnosed dissociative identity disorder, although further testing is needed."

Dissociative identity disorder. The term hung in Rachel's mind like an echo. She knew Eli was cautious about leaning on a DID diagnosis, especially in a court of law. But the more she uncovered about Emily, the more convinced she became that her client's mind had been a battlefield for years—a mind forced to fracture to survive.

Rachel's thoughts drifted to a story Emily had shared in their first meeting, an almost childlike recollection of her favourite hiding spot growing up. "It was a closet, just big enough for me to crawl inside. I'd stay there for hours, close my eyes, and imagine I was somewhere else." Rachel had sensed a sadness in Emily's voice, an attempt to rewrite her reality by disappearing into a safer mental space.

But now, with these reports in hand, Rachel wondered if Emily's "safe space" had turned into something darker—something beyond her control.

As the morning wore on, Rachel found herself imagining what Emily's mind might look like, piece by piece. She could almost envision a hallway of closed doors, each one leading to a different memory or fragment of her identity. She wondered if Emily had ever tried to open one of those doors herself or if she'd simply shut them tight, refusing to face the contents within.

Rachel's focus shifted as she came across a final report, one filed by a caseworker who'd visited Emily during her teenage years. She skimmed through it, until a specific line stopped her cold:

"Emily often speaks of feeling like an 'observer' in her own life, describing herself as two people: one who feels, and one who watches. Possible indicators of dissociative experiences. Mother denies therapy for financial reasons, though daughter exhibits signs of acute distress."

Rachel could practically hear the young girl's voice, describing the feeling of being outside herself, like a shadow trailing behind her body, observing without participating. It was a common trait of dissociation—a coping mechanism that allowed the mind to detach from the pain of reality.

Rachel's stomach clenched as she envisioned Emily's life through the cold, impersonal language of these reports. She imagined the fear that must have gripped Emily as a child, forcing her mind to split off, creating new layers, each one more distant from reality than the last.

Rachel closed the file, leaning back in her chair. She took a deep breath, trying to settle her racing thoughts. The past had left its fingerprints all over Emily's mind, fingerprints she'd been forced to cover and hide. But there was one question Rachel couldn't shake:

Had Emily ever committed violence in one of her dissociative states? And if so…, was she truly responsible?

The knock at her door broke her reverie. Eli stepped in, taking a seat across from her, his expression serious.

"What did you find?" he asked, his eyes flicking to the thick file in front of her.

Rachel pushed the folder toward him, letting the weight of Emily's past land between them. "This," she said quietly. "A lifetime of trauma, abuse, dissociative episodes… it's all there. She's been through more than anyone could imagine, and it's scarred her. Fractured her, even."

Eli's expression softened as he took the folder, flipping through the pages, his gaze hardening with each new discovery. "No wonder she dissociates," he murmured. "It's a survival tactic. Her mind had to fracture to survive."

Rachel nodded, glancing away. "But Eli, if that's true, then this isn't just about defending her against murder charges. It's about defending a mind that's been shattered by trauma."

Eli leaned back, rubbing his chin thoughtfully. "This changes things, Rachel. If she truly has DID—or even a complex form of dissociation—it could mean she wasn't fully aware of her actions. But the courts won't be easy to convince. We'd be asking them to view her mind as a crime scene, one where she herself is both the victim and potential threat."

Rachel closed her eyes, absorbing the magnitude of what he'd just said. Emily wasn't simply a defendant. She was a person who'd been wounded so deeply that her mind had reshaped itself to keep her alive. And now, that fractured mind had led her here, to a cold holding cell, under suspicion for a murder she might not even remember committing.

"This case isn't just about Emily's innocence," Rachel murmured, her voice tinged with a fierce resolve. "It's about proving that a mind can be broken by others—and that sometimes, the person responsible for a crime isn't always the person holding the weapon."

Eli nodded slowly, his gaze intent. "Then let's get to work," he said, his voice calm but determined. "If anyone can bring her truth to light, it's us."

Rachel felt a surge of resolve, the weight of Emily's story settling within her as both a burden and a mission. She knew that their journey into Emily's fractured mind would be treacherous, filled with shadows and questions that might never fully resolve.

But one thing was certain: they wouldn't stop until they'd uncovered the truth, even if that truth shattered everything, they thought they knew about justice, responsibility, and the depths of the human mind.

Chapter 4: The First Court Appearance

The courtroom was a powder keg, each murmured voice like a spark waiting to ignite. Journalists lined the back rows, their cameras poised like weapons, each flash promising a new headline, a fresh slant. Rachel could feel the tension buzzing in the air, thick with the scent of judgment and anticipation. She adjusted her collar, straightened her papers, and glanced over at Emily, seated next to her with vacant eyes that drifted, unfocused, around the room.

Emily looked small and fragile under the harsh fluorescent lights; her hands clasped tightly in her lap. She seemed almost translucent, a wisp of a person who didn't belong among the dark wood and cold metal of the courtroom. For Rachel, this only underscored the strangeness of the situation—this young woman, so removed from violence and intent, accused of such a savage crime.

The bailiff announced the judge's arrival, and the room fell silent. Judge Hayes entered, a formidable figure whose reputation for fairness was matched only by his intolerance for theatrics. He took his seat, eyes scanning the courtroom with a mixture of scepticism and gravity.

As the proceedings began, Rachel's mind raced through the strategy she'd spent days refining. She was fighting for bail, something that felt as elusive as the truth in this case. The prosecutor, David Rourke, had made it clear he intended to use every tool at his disposal to keep Emily locked up—and Rachel knew he'd succeed if she wasn't prepared to counter each of his points with precision.

Rourke rose first, his figure tall and imposing as he addressed the court with a deliberate solemnity. He wore the mantle of justice with practiced ease, his tone resonant with conviction as he outlined the reasons for denying bail.

"Your Honor," Rourke began, "we are here today because of a crime that has shocked this community. Emily Grant was found at the scene, her hands bloodied, standing over the body of her husband. This was no simple domestic dispute; it was an act of extreme violence, an act that indicates a deep-seated anger and instability."

He paused, letting the words settle like stones into the silence, each one weighted with purpose. Rachel felt her jaw tighten, her fingers flexing over her notes. She could feel the crowd shifting, a ripple of indignation as Rourke painted a picture of Emily as a dangerous woman. He was playing on their fears, using the public's discomfort with mental illness to his advantage. And from the quiet nods and whispers, it was working.

Rourke continued, "We have evidence linking Mrs. Grant to the crime. DNA, fingerprints, a weapon left in plain sight. This was a brutal, calculated act. It's clear that she poses a risk—not only to others but to herself. To grant bail would be to disregard the safety of this community and the gravity of her crime."

Rachel felt a pang in her chest as Rourke emphasized the word "calculated." The entire foundation of her defence rested on the idea that Emily hadn't been in her right mind, that she hadn't fully understood her actions. But Rourke was spinning a different narrative, one in which Emily was a cold-blooded killer, a threat to society.

When Rourke finally sat down, Rachel stood, feeling every pair of eyes shift onto her. She took a steadying breath, gathering her thoughts before she spoke.

"Your Honor, while the charges against my client are indeed serious, I urge the court to consider her circumstances. Emily Grant has no prior criminal record, and she's lived her entire life without so much as a speeding ticket. She has been a peaceful, law-abiding citizen."

Rachel felt the weight of her words settle in the room. She saw Judge Hayes watching her, his gaze sharp but not unfriendly. There was a flicker of interest in his eyes, as if he were waiting to see if she could sway him.

"My client has a documented history of dissociative episodes," Rachel continued, her voice strong. "We believe that her mental state at the time of the incident was compromised, that she was not in control of her actions. She has cooperated fully with the investigation, and I assure this court that she poses no danger if released on bail."

But as Rachel spoke, she could feel the resistance in the room, a wall of doubt pressing back against her words. She glanced over at Rourke, who was leaning back, his arms folded across his chest, a slight smirk playing at his lips. He was confident, secure in the public sentiment that had already condemned Emily in the court of opinion.

Judge Hayes considered Rachel's argument, tapping his gavel lightly against the bench. "Ms. Yates," he said, his tone careful, "while I respect your client's cooperation, I can't overlook the violent nature of this crime. The evidence points to a very clear and immediate threat."

Rachel felt a pang of frustration but kept her expression calm, knowing any sign of weakness would only fuel Rourke's narrative.

"Your Honor, I understand the severity of the allegations," she replied. "But I urge you to consider the unique aspects of Emily's mental health. With respect, she requires care and evaluation, not punishment."

Judge Hayes leaned forward, his eyes narrowing as he weighed her words. There was a long pause, a silence that seemed to stretch, filling the room with a tense expectation.

Then, he spoke, his tone firm. "Ms. Yates, I am sympathetic to your argument, but given the severity of the charges and the substantial evidence presented by the prosecution, I must deny bail at this time."

Rachel felt the floor drop out from under her. Emily's eyes widened, her gaze darting to Rachel in panic, but Rachel reached out, gently placing a hand on her arm. She could feel the tremors racing through Emily's body, a physical manifestation of the fear that had taken root within her.

As they prepared to leave, a murmur broke out in the back rows, reporters already scrambling to type out headlines that would scream Emily's guilt. Rachel knew this was only the beginning, but the implications of Judge Hayes's decision loomed large.

Later, back in her office, Rachel sat with Eli, the tension of the day still hanging between them. Eli was silent, his fingers tapping rhythmically on the table as he processed the day's events. Rachel could see the weight of the case reflected in his eyes, a mixture of doubt and determination.

"They're framing her as a monster," Rachel murmured, breaking the silence. "No one wants to see her as a victim. To them, she's already guilty."

Eli sighed, leaning back in his chair. "It's an uphill battle, no doubt. The court won't be easily convinced of her innocence—especially not with dissociation as her defence. People don't want to understand the complexities of mental illness; they want simple answers, someone to blame."

Rachel nodded, feeling a surge of frustration rise within her. "And Rourke's feeding that. He's using their fear, their discomfort with the unknown, to his advantage. They'll never see her as a person as long as he keeps framing her as a monster."

Eli's gaze softened, his voice steady as he replied, "Then it's our job to change that. To show them who Emily really is, to force them to look beyond the headlines and the fear."

Rachel exhaled slowly, nodding. She could feel the gravity of Eli's words, the weight of the task that lay before them. This case would be a battle, not only for Emily's freedom but for her humanity.

And as she looked out the window at the darkening sky, Rachel knew that this was only the beginning. The public's judgment would only intensify, their voices growing louder as the trial approached. She could almost hear the whispers, the rumours that would spread, painting Emily as a villain in a story where she was little more than a pawn.

But Rachel wouldn't back down. She was more determined than ever to fight for Emily, to stand between her and a world that had already decided her fate. And with Eli by her side, she knew they had a chance—a slim one, perhaps, but a chance nonetheless—to turn the tide, to reveal the truth buried beneath the layers of fear and misunderstanding.

As the clock struck midnight, Rachel closed her files, her mind still racing. She knew the road ahead would be long, filled with doubt and darkness. But she was prepared to fight, to shine a light into the shadows, and to prove that even in a world of harsh judgments and unyielding labels, justice could still be found.

Chapter 5: Uncovering Secrets

The interview room at the detention centre was cold, almost sterile. The white walls were unblemished, save for a faint water stain in one corner, as if some forgotten leak had left its mark. Eli adjusted his notes, setting his pen and recorder on the table in front of him, ready to begin. He had conducted countless interviews before, each one unique, each subject an enigma, but something about Emily Grant set his nerves on edge. He didn't believe in premonitions, yet the hairs on his arms prickled with an almost supernatural awareness.

A guard escorted Emily into the room, her steps hesitant, like a child unsure of her surroundings. She was small, dwarfed by the oversized prison clothes, and her shoulders slumped as if the very act of carrying her own weight was an ordeal. She glanced at Eli briefly, her gaze flitting away as soon as he met her eyes.

"Thank you, Officer," Eli said, and the guard left them alone, the heavy door clicking shut with a resounding finality.

"Emily," Eli greeted, keeping his tone gentle but direct. "How are you feeling today?"

She paused, her expression shifting, a flicker of uncertainty passing over her face. "I don't know. I feel…off. Like there's a fog in my head, and I can't clear it." Her fingers twisted together in her lap, knuckles turning white from the pressure.

Eli leaned forward slightly, gauging her reaction. "Let's try to work through that fog, okay? Take your time. I'm here to help."

Emily nodded, though her movements were stiff, almost mechanical. He could tell she was holding back, as if she'd learned somewhere along the way that opening up only led to more pain. With trauma patients, it was often a matter of patience and persistence, finding that delicate balance between digging for the truth and pushing too hard.

"Emily, I want to talk about that night," Eli began, watching her closely. "I know it's difficult, but I want to understand what happened. Anything you remember, even if it doesn't make sense, could be helpful."

Her body stiffened, and her eyes glazed over, her breath coming in shallow, uneven gulps. Eli held up a hand, cautioning her to slow down.

"Take a deep breath," he said softly. "There's no rush. Just let yourself relax."

Emily swallowed, her gaze unfocused, as if she were looking beyond him, seeing something he couldn't. Her lips parted, but no words came out. Eli waited, feeling the tension build, sensing that she was on the edge of something—a memory, a revelation, or perhaps a barrier her mind had erected to protect her from the truth.

"I…remember the blood," she finally whispered, her voice trembling. "I remember the smell, and…my hands…they were covered in it."

Her voice was barely audible, and she shuddered, wrapping her arms around herself as if to shield herself from the horror of her own words. Eli felt a pang of sympathy. There was no mistaking the genuine terror in her voice, the confusion etched into every line of her face.

"Emily, do you remember anything before that? Anything that led up to that moment?"

She shook her head, her brow furrowing as if she were struggling to reach back through the fog that clouded her mind. "It's…blank. I know I was there, but it's like watching a movie, like it happened to someone else."

Eli nodded, jotting down notes. Dissociation was common in trauma survivors, but her case seemed more severe than he'd anticipated. She wasn't just distancing herself from the memory; it was as if she'd fragmented, leaving pieces of herself behind.

"Emily, I'm going to ask you something, and I want you to answer as best as you can, even if it feels strange or doesn't seem to make sense. Have you ever felt like…someone else was in control?"

Her eyes darted to his, wide and fearful. She looked away quickly, her hands tightening on the edge of the table. "I…I don't know what you mean."

"Sometimes," Eli continued gently, "when people experience severe trauma, their minds develop ways to cope. Some people feel like they become different versions of themselves. Have you ever felt like that?"

A long silence followed. He could see the internal struggle, the war waging in her mind as she fought against an invisible force. And then, almost imperceptibly, something shifted.

Her body language changed, her posture straightening as she looked him directly in the eyes, her expression unreadable. Eli held his breath, sensing that whoever was now facing him wasn't the same woman who had walked in.

"What do you want?" she asked, her voice colder, sharper, a complete departure from the timid Emily he'd been speaking to moments before.

The transformation was startling. Gone was the frightened woman, replaced by someone who seemed almost…defiant.

"Emily?" he asked cautiously, though he knew the answer was more complex than that.

"No," she replied, a faint smile playing at her lips, a bitter twist of amusement. "Emily's not here right now. She's…resting."

Eli felt a chill run down his spine. Dissociative Identity Disorder. He'd suspected it, but seeing it unfold in front of him was another matter entirely. He steadied his breathing, reminding himself to remain calm.

"Who am I speaking to?" he asked, his tone as measured as he could manage.

"Names aren't important," she replied, a shadow flickering in her gaze. "What's important is that you understand Emily doesn't belong here. She was never strong enough to handle what life threw at her. That's why I exist."

Eli scribbled furiously, his mind racing to absorb the implications of what he was hearing. This wasn't just a case of simple dissociation. Emily had compartmentalized parts of herself, splitting off into different versions—each one a response to her past traumas.

"Why don't you tell me more?" he said, keeping his tone as neutral as possible. "What is it that you do for Emily?"

A small laugh escaped her—a hollow, mirthless sound. "I protect her. I keep her safe from things she's too weak to face. I do what she can't, or won't. And sometimes…that means making difficult decisions."

Eli's pulse quickened, but he kept his expression carefully blank. "What kind of decisions?"

Her gaze turned distant, almost wistful, as if remembering something from a dream. "Decisions that let her sleep at night. Decisions that keep the nightmares at bay."

He felt a knot tighten in his stomach. This alter—whoever she was—seemed to view herself as Emily's shield, someone who emerged only when Emily couldn't cope. But what exactly did she protect Emily from?

"Do you remember the night of the incident?" he asked, carefully phrasing his question.

The woman's face hardened. "I remember enough. Enough to know that Emily couldn't handle it. She was slipping, losing control. I had to step in."

Eli swallowed, piecing together the fragments of what she was telling him. It was as if this part of Emily's mind had taken over, acting in ways Emily either couldn't remember or couldn't bear to acknowledge.

"Are you the one who…hurt him?" Eli ventured, his voice barely above a whisper.

The woman leaned back, crossing her arms with a casualness that was at odds with the severity of the question. "What does it matter? He deserved it. He always deserved it."

The venom in her voice was chilling, and Eli felt his heart pounding in his chest. Whoever this alter was, she was fiercely protective of Emily, almost to a fault.

But what kind of protector took a life?

"Why don't you tell me about him?" Eli pressed gently. "About what he did to Emily."

Her expression darkened, her lips twisting into a sneer. "He was cruel. Cruel in ways Emily couldn't see, couldn't understand. But I saw. I felt every insult, every hurt. He broke her, piece by piece. And I…was there to pick up those pieces."

The confession hung in the air, thick with implications. Eli's pen hovered above his notebook, his mind racing to interpret the layers of trauma that had led Emily to this point. This alter, this defensive part of her, had risen in response to suffering, taking on the role of protector by any means necessary.

Eli leaned forward, his voice calm but firm. "Emily deserves to be heard, and so do you. But you're going to have to help me understand—if I'm to help her, I need to know what happened, what drove you to act."

The woman's gaze softened, a trace of vulnerability surfacing beneath her defiance. "Emily can't remember. But I remember everything. Every pain, every slight, every cruel word. He took away her peace. So, I took away his."

With that, she fell silent, her gaze growing unfocused once more. The shift was subtle, but Eli could sense the change as Emily's alter receded, leaving the room silent and heavy with the weight of what had just unfolded.

When Emily finally looked up, her face was blank, her eyes wide with confusion. She had no memory of what had transpired, no recollection of the confession that hung in the air like a shadow.

Eli closed his notebook, feeling the weight of the truth pressing down on him. This case was more complex, more tangled than he'd ever imagined, and the stakes had just grown unimaginably high.

Chapter 6: The First Thread

Rachel Yates sat at her desk, files and photos splayed out before her, lit only by the dim, flickering light of her office lamp. The rest of the firm was silent, the kind of stillness that only settled in after midnight, when even the cleaning staff had finished for the day. She massaged her temples, eyes skimming over her notes for what felt like the hundredth time, each detail unravelling new questions rather than answers.

Emily Grant. Husband dead, her hands drenched in blood, yet her memory splintered into a fog of forgetfulness and fear. Rachel had seen many things in her years as a defence attorney, but this case clawed at her mind in a way she couldn't quite explain. Perhaps it was the sheer impossibility of it all—how Emily seemed to be both the most vulnerable victim and the most obvious suspect.

But it was more than that.

Rachel's eyes drifted to a clipping she'd pulled from her archives. A photograph of another woman, another husband, a similar scene from seven years ago. There was something familiar in the setup—a disturbed young woman standing over the body of her husband, her memory fractured, her story riddled with gaps. She frowned, feeling the threads of an idea beginning to weave together.

It was a long shot, a very long shot, but Rachel knew better than to ignore her instincts. She grabbed her phone, pulling up a contact she hadn't dialled in years.

The phone rang twice before a gravelly voice answered, "Detective King here."

"Detective, it's Rachel Yates."

There was a pause, a moment of static-filled recognition. "Rachel. Been a long time."

"It has. I wish I could say this was a social call."

"Something tells me it's not. You only reach out when you're on a case that's…tricky," he replied with a knowing chuckle. "So, what's got you calling at one in the morning?"

Rachel took a deep breath. "Do you remember the Monica Lowell case? Seven years ago. Husband killed; wife found at the scene with no memory of what happened."

"Lowell…" Detective King's voice grew thoughtful. "Yeah, I remember. We could never pin it on her, and she ended up in a psych facility. Claimed she didn't remember a thing, just like you're saying. Weird case."

"That's the one. I'm working on a new case, and the similarities…well, they're eerie."

"You're not saying you think they're connected, are you?"

"Maybe," Rachel replied cautiously. "Maybe not directly, but I can't shake the feeling that there's something we're missing, something bigger."

Detective King hesitated. "I'll see what I can pull up, but don't get too deep in the weeds with this. You know as well as I do that coincidences happen, especially in high-stress cases. Sometimes it's just that—coincidence."

"Right. But I'd still like to look into it."

"Sure, Rachel. I'll send over whatever I've got."

As she hung up, Rachel felt a surge of adrenaline course through her. It wasn't much, but it was a lead—a fragile thread that, if tugged just right, might unravel something hidden beneath the surface of Emily's case.

The next day, Rachel shared her suspicions with Eli as they sat across from each other in a small café near the courthouse. Eli listened in silence, his expression unreadable, occasionally sipping his coffee as she laid out her theory.

"You think this other case is connected," he said finally, his voice level.

"I think there's a pattern," Rachel replied. "Two women, both suffering from memory issues, both found standing over their husbands' bodies without any explanation for what happened. And both with pasts riddled with trauma and psychological issues. There's something here, Eli."

Eli raised an eyebrow, his tone shifting to that of a cautious sceptic. "Rachel, patterns can be dangerous. You know as well as I do that when we start looking for connections, we're more likely to find them—even if they don't exist. It's called confirmation bias."

She rolled her eyes. "I know what confirmation bias is, Eli. But that doesn't mean I'm wrong. Think about it—if Emily's mental health issues were so extreme that they led to an alter taking over, maybe it's not that unique. Maybe someone out there knows how to push these women into a breaking point, triggering these episodes for their own reasons."

Eli set his cup down, considering her words. "It's a fascinating theory, but without evidence, it's just that—a theory. And theories don't hold up in court."

Rachel felt a spark of irritation, but she pushed it down, knowing he was right. "Fine. Then help me find the evidence. The last thing I want is to present some wild idea in court without anything concrete to back it up. But if we start digging—"

He held up a hand. "If we start digging, we risk finding things we can't unsee. Rachel, if you're right, and there's some orchestrated reason behind these deaths, we could be dealing with something dangerous. We need to tread carefully."

She met his gaze, her expression fierce. "We've never backed down from a challenge before, Eli. And I'm not about to start now."

Later that day, as Rachel combed through case records and old news articles, she found herself wondering if Eli might be right. She'd felt so certain about the connection, but the more she read, the more tangled the threads became. The cases were eerily similar, yes, but the question of *how* and *why* lingered like a shadow.

Just as she was about to give up for the day, an email from Detective King popped into her inbox. She opened it eagerly, her eyes scanning the brief note he'd attached:

Rachel, here's what I could find from the Lowell case. There's a psychiatric assessment you might want to read. Says something about dissociative states and a history of violent episodes in her youth. Sound familiar? Take care, and be careful. This one's tricky. - King

Rachel opened the attached file and began reading through the psychiatric report. The assessment was hauntingly familiar, detailing Monica Lowell's struggles with dissociation, her memory lapses, her feelings of losing control. It mirrored Emily's condition almost perfectly, even down to the timing of her episodes—each triggered by moments of intense emotional stress, often brought on by her husband's behaviour.

Her heart pounded as she continued reading. There, buried near the end of the document, was a statement Monica had made during one of her more lucid moments, as if she were speaking to someone unseen:

"He said he could make it all go away. He promised I'd be free."

Rachel's blood ran cold. The words were cryptic, but something about them felt all too real. Who was "he"? And what had he promised Monica?

Just as she was piecing together this disturbing detail, her phone buzzed. It was Eli.

"I've been thinking about what you said earlier," he began without preamble. "I want to try something with Emily. It might help us understand her alters better, see if we can get her to remember more about the night of the murder."

Rachel's heart leaped at the thought. "You think it'll work?"

"Maybe. But it's risky. If her mind is fractured as we suspect, asking her to relive those moments could either help her piece things together—or drive her deeper into dissociation."

Rachel's mind raced, weighing the risks and rewards. "Let's do it. I'll be there to help if things go south."

Two days later, they met in the interview room, with Emily sitting nervously between them, her hands clenched tightly in her lap. Eli spoke in his calm, measured tone, explaining that they were going to ask her a series of questions and that she should answer them as best she could.

Emily nodded, though her face was pale, her eyes darting nervously between them.

"Emily," Eli began, his voice soothing, "I want you to think back to the night of the incident. I know it's hard, but I'm here to help you. Can you tell me what you remember?"

She hesitated, biting her lip, but then a distant look filled her eyes as she sank into herself, a kind of trance. "I…remember a voice," she murmured, her tone detached. "Someone saying they could help me, that they could make it all go away."

Eli shot Rachel a quick, meaningful glance. "Emily, who was it? Who said that?"

She blinked, her eyes cloudy, as if she were watching a memory unfold in slow motion. "I don't know. I didn't see his face. Just his voice…calm, steady, like he'd done this before."

Rachel felt a chill settle over the room. Could there truly be someone out there, manipulating women like Emily and Monica, driving them to the brink for reasons she couldn't yet fathom?

Eli's voice was gentle but insistent. "Emily, do you remember anything else? Anything specific about him?"

Emily shuddered, wrapping her arms around herself. "He said…he said he'd come back, that I'd know when it was time. And then…everything went dark."

Rachel swallowed, feeling the weight of Emily's words settle over her like a storm cloud. Whoever was behind this, whoever had preyed on Monica and now Emily, was out there, watching, waiting.

And Rachel was determined to find him, no matter what it took.

Chapter 7: A Revelation from the Past

Rachel sat in her office, the early morning light filtering through the blinds and casting long shadows over her desk. The discovery from Emily's interview still buzzed in her mind—a voice, a man, promising he could make things "go away." The words felt insidious, laced with a kind of cruelty that Rachel couldn't shake. Who was this man, and how had he managed to push women like Emily and Monica to the very edge?

Lost in thought, she barely heard the knock on her door. Eli stepped inside; his face lined with fatigue but his eyes sharp with purpose.

"Rachel," he said, taking a seat across from her. "I've been going through some additional files on Emily's husband, Derek Grant. There's something you need to see."

He placed a thick file on her desk, neatly labelled with Derek's name. Rachel frowned, flipping through the pages. Derek's face stared back at her from a faded photograph, his expression cold, almost clinical. She couldn't shake the chill that ran down her spine as she studied him. There was something off about him, even in the stillness of the photo.

"Derek was more than just a psychiatrist," Eli explained, his voice a quiet murmur. "He had a reputation in certain circles as…well, someone who pushed boundaries. He was known for his interest in dissociative identity disorder, or DID. But his colleagues described his methods as extreme, even unethical."

Rachel's brow furrowed as she skimmed the reports, each line confirming her worst fears. "You're saying he experimented on her?"

Eli nodded. "There's evidence to suggest that Derek may have been conducting his own kind of psychological tests on Emily, under the pretence of treatment. He could have been using her dissociative episodes to study how far he could push her mind, to see if he could deliberately trigger her alters. He may have even been trying to create new ones."

Rachel's stomach turned. "That's monstrous," she whispered. "He was her husband. How could he do that to her?"

Eli shook his head. "We're talking about someone who saw people as puzzles to be solved, not individuals with real lives and emotions. For Derek, Emily might have been a fascinating subject first and a wife second—if at all."

Rachel closed her eyes, letting the weight of Eli's words sink in. Every new detail seemed to paint a darker picture of the life Emily had endured. And the more they uncovered, the more Rachel began to understand the complexity of Emily's trauma.

"What exactly did he do to her, Eli?"

Eli leaned back; his gaze distant. "According to his notes—and they're extensive, Rachel—Derek used techniques designed to destabilize her sense of self. He kept her isolated, limited her interactions with friends and family, and undermined her reality at every turn. She was forced to rely on him entirely. The more she depended on him, the more control he had."

Rachel felt a surge of anger build in her chest. "So, he groomed her. He systematically broke her down."

"Yes. And I believe he went a step further," Eli continued, his voice grim. "Derek took advantage of Emily's dissociative episodes to shape her mind, as though he were conditioning her. He may have even implanted suggestions or memories, guiding her actions in a way she wouldn't be aware of. Her alters may have been formed as a direct response to Derek's so-called treatments."

Rachel's mind reeled. "These changes everything," she murmured, pacing her office as her thoughts raced. "We're no longer talking about a woman who simply snapped. Emily was deliberately conditioned, controlled to a horrifying extent."

"But can we prove it?" Eli asked, a shadow of doubt in his voice.

"That's the real question, isn't it?" Rachel said, chewing her lip. "If we can prove Derek manipulated Emily, that he drove her to the point of no return…then we can argue that she's as much a victim as he is."

Eli tapped his fingers thoughtfully on the desk. "Derek was meticulous, Rachel. If there's proof of what he did, it's hidden somewhere we haven't looked yet."

Rachel's mind worked, sifting through the options. "Maybe his clinic. If he kept any recordings, notes, or evidence, that's where it would be. But the clinic closed after his death, didn't it?"

"It did," Eli confirmed. "But someone would have had access to his records. His assistant, perhaps. Or one of his colleagues who shared his…enthusiasm for alternative methods."

"Then that's our next step," Rachel decided. "I'll contact the clinic's last known administrator and see if they have anything on file. We need to find that evidence, Eli. Emily's life may depend on it."

Later that day, Rachel and Eli visited the now-abandoned clinic where Derek had once conducted his questionable practices. The place had an eerie silence, as if the walls still held whispers of the things that had happened there. They walked through the dim corridors, their footsteps echoing in the empty space.

Eli stopped outside Derek's former office, his hand resting on the doorknob. "Are you ready for this?"

Rachel nodded, though her pulse quickened. Inside, the office was a time capsule of Derek's life—a tidy desk, empty filing cabinets, and shelves lined with psychology textbooks and reference materials. It was as though he'd just stepped out, leaving behind only traces of his presence.

Eli began rummaging through the desk drawers while Rachel examined the bookshelf, her fingers running over the titles. One particular book caught her eye, a thick volume on abnormal psychology that seemed well-worn. She pulled it from the shelf, surprised to find a loose page tucked between its covers.

Rachel unfolded the paper, her heart pounding as she read the notes scrawled across it in Derek's handwriting. The words were clinical, detached, a list of observations and assessments that felt more like data points than a record of a human being.

Patient E.G., Day 57. Severe dissociative episodes continue under stress-inducing conditions. Suggestive conditioning appears effective—altered state responds to specific triggers.

Rachel's blood ran cold as she realized the initials were Emily's. These weren't just notes; they were Derek's own observations of his manipulations. The document was essentially a blueprint of his psychological control over her.

Eli peered over her shoulder, his face darkening as he read. "This is damning evidence, Rachel. This could prove that Derek was conditioning Emily, deliberately pushing her into states where she'd have no control."

"But we need more," Rachel murmured, glancing around the office. "This proves his intention, but if we're going to convince a jury, we need hard evidence. Recordings, reports, anything."

Eli nodded, his eyes scanning the room with renewed focus. They searched every inch, finally uncovering a locked drawer in the desk. Rachel gave it a gentle tug, but it didn't budge.

"It's locked," she said, frustrated.

Eli produced a small screwdriver from his pocket, giving her a wry smile. "Old investigator's trick. Let me give it a shot."

With a few deft movements, he pried the drawer open, revealing a small, battered cassette recorder inside. Rachel's heart leapt as she pulled it out, examining it closely. It looked like it hadn't been touched in years, but it was in good enough condition to potentially hold Derek's voice, or worse, Emily's.

"Do you think it still works?" she asked, almost afraid of the answer.

Eli shrugged. "Only one way to find out."

They made their way back to Rachel's office, where she plugged in an old set of headphones and pressed play. A moment of static filled her ears, then Derek's voice broke through, calm and steady.

"Session 13. Patient E.G. displaying expected signs of dissociation. Trigger word 'solace' applied. Patient assumes submissive posture, responds compliantly."

Rachel's stomach twisted as she listened, unable to tear herself away from the sickening details. Derek's tone was cold, clinical, as though he were discussing a science experiment rather than his own wife.

But the worst part came when she heard Emily's voice, fragile and distant, as if coming from somewhere far away. She sounded disoriented, repeating words Derek fed to her, her tone hollow.

"Solace," she whispered on the tape, her voice breaking slightly. "I…feel safe. I feel nothing."

Rachel ripped the headphones off, unable to bear it any longer. Eli watched her, his face lined with worry.

"That tape is horrifying, Rachel. But it's exactly what we need. Proof that Derek manipulated her, drove her to the brink of insanity."

Rachel nodded, her hands trembling. "We can use this to build our case, show the jury that Emily wasn't in control of her actions because of him. He took away her free will."

Eli placed a reassuring hand on her shoulder. "It's a dark revelation, but it's a revelation that can change everything for Emily. You've done well to find this, Rachel."

She took a deep breath, steadying herself. "This is only the beginning, Eli. We're going to bring the truth to light, no matter how much darkness we have to face to get there."

They both sat in silence, aware that they had just uncovered a piece of the puzzle—a key to unravelling the psychological chains that had bound Emily. But with each revelation came a deeper descent into Derek's twisted mind and the reality Emily had been forced to endure.

Chapter 8: Pressure Mounts

The media frenzy surrounding Emily Grant's case was nothing short of a spectacle. The first article had appeared within hours of her arrest, but now, as the weeks went on, the headlines were a relentless barrage. Every news outlet, every morning show, every tabloid had found their new villain: Emily Grant, the "dangerous woman" who had allegedly killed her husband in cold blood.

Rachel couldn't escape it, no matter where she went. On the way to her office, a headline flashed across the screen of a nearby newsstand: **"The Killer Who Uses Dissociation as a Defence: Emily Grant's 'Psychotic Break'—Or a Cold-Blooded Murderer?"**

It wasn't just the media. Social media had erupted, with hashtags like **#JusticeForDerek** trending alongside **#FreeEmily**, which, ironically, was less about support and more about the emotional tug-of-war. Some were convinced that Emily was guilty and the mental illness defence was just another manipulation. Others argued that she was just another victim of a flawed system, trapped in a web of abuse and trauma.

Everywhere Rachel went, she could feel the eyes on her. Whispered conversations. Muffled laughter. Judgments made before a verdict was ever reached. It was as though Emily had already been convicted in the court of public opinion—and Rachel, as her defender, had become an easy target.

She tried to keep her focus on the case. She had to. But the pressure was mounting on all sides. The prosecution was gaining momentum, the media was vilifying her client, and even some of Rachel's colleagues had started to distance themselves from her.

"Rachel, are you sure you want to take this case any further?" That was Paul's voice, one of the senior partners at the firm. He stood by her office door, his arms crossed, a concerned expression on his face.

"I'm not backing down," she said, her voice firm. "I believe in Emily's innocence."

Paul sighed; his expression tinged with frustration. "I'm not saying she's guilty, Rachel. But this case is a PR nightmare. It's already blown up. The firm is getting calls from the media, from our clients. We're under a microscope. People are questioning your judgment."

"People who don't know the truth," she replied, her gaze fixed on the file in front of her, her fingers brushing over the stack of evidence. "I have to do what's right. I can't let the public opinion or their anger dictate my decisions."

"You might not have a choice," Paul muttered before turning to leave, his voice carrying an undercurrent of finality. "Just think about it."

Rachel wasn't sure if it was Paul's words or the weight of the public's judgment that made her feel more isolated. She had spent years defending clients in cases where the stakes were high, but this felt different. She had always believed that the law existed to protect the innocent, to give everyone a fair chance—even those who had been branded as monsters by the world. But now, as the media painted Emily as a cold-blooded killer, Rachel's faith in the system was being tested in ways she hadn't anticipated.

The courthouse was a battlefield, and the public's anger had become its ammunition.

Rachel arrived early the next morning for another pre-trial hearing. The crowds had gathered outside the building, a sea of cameras and microphones, all pointed in her direction. They were like sharks circling in the water, waiting for any sign of weakness. Reporters shouted questions at her as she made her way through the crowd, her face steeled in determination, but her insides were anything but calm.

"Rachel! How can you defend a woman who might be guilty of murder?" a reporter called out.

"Is your client really as unstable as she appears?" another shouted.

"Do you really believe Emily Grant deserves a defence?" a third pressed.

Rachel ignored the barrage of questions, forcing herself to stay focused on the task at hand. She had a job to do. The cameras weren't her concern—not right now. She was here for one person, and that person was Emily.

Inside the courthouse, the tension was palpable. Rachel could feel the weight of every stare as she walked through the halls, her presence almost tangible. Even the judges, the clerks, the other lawyers—everyone knew who she was, knew what case she was handling, and more importantly, knew the public outcry surrounding it.

Her thoughts were interrupted by a knock at her office door. Eli entered; his face drawn with concern.

"I heard the latest," Eli said, sitting down across from Rachel. "It's bad. I've never seen the press go after a defence attorney like this before."

Rachel rubbed her temples, feeling the pressure in her chest tighten. "It's getting worse. I can't go anywhere without hearing people whisper about me. They're calling me unethical for taking Emily's case. They're calling her a murderer before she's even had a chance to defend herself."

Eli leaned back in his chair; his eyes thoughtful. "I knew it would get ugly. But I think you're doing the right thing. You have to keep your focus on Emily. The rest of the world will see what they want to see, but you know the truth. And that truth will come out."

"I hope so," Rachel said, but the doubt lingered in her voice. She had always prided herself on standing firm in the face of adversity, but this was something new. Something she hadn't been prepared for. Emily's fate was no longer in her hands alone. It was tied to public opinion, to the media's portrayal of her, to every emotional appeal made to a jury that might already be swayed before the trial had even begun.

As they headed toward the courtroom for the hearing, Rachel couldn't shake the feeling that the stakes were higher than ever before. If they lost this pre-trial motion—if bail was denied again, or worse, if the media continued to demonize Emily—there might be no coming back.

The prosecutor, a tall man with sharp features named Gregory Reid, was already seated at the front of the courtroom when Rachel and Eli entered. He was scanning through his notes, not even looking up as they took their seats. His confidence was undeniable. He knew how to work the room, how to control the narrative, and his calm demeanour only made him more dangerous.

Rachel's eyes flicked over to the gallery. There was a noticeable number of spectators—mostly reporters, but there were a few curious faces too. She caught the eyes of a woman in the front row who stared at her with disdain. Rachel didn't know if the woman was a supporter of Emily or just another part of the public's mob mentality, but it didn't matter. Emily's fate had become a public spectacle, and Rachel was at the centre of it.

Judge Thornton, a middle-aged man with a reputation for being tough but fair, called the hearing to order. His gaze lingered on Rachel as he adjusted his glasses, a sign that he, too, was well aware of the media frenzy surrounding the case.

"Ms. Yates, you're here today to request a reconsideration of the bail denial," Judge Thornton said, his voice firm.

Rachel stood, feeling the weight of his scrutiny. She cleared her throat and addressed the court.

"Yes, Your Honor. I'm requesting that the court reconsider the denial of bail for my client, Emily Grant. She has no prior criminal history, she is not a flight risk, and she has strong ties to the community. The conditions of her arrest were not in line with the severity of the charges, and I believe she deserves the opportunity to be released while we prepare her defence."

The prosecutor, Reid, stood up quickly, his voice cutting through the air. "Your Honor, with all due respect, the nature of the crime is far too brutal to allow bail. Emily Grant is a danger to society. She stands accused of killing her husband, and the evidence—while circumstantial—is damning. The court has already seen the photographs of the crime scene, and the defendant's behaviour following the incident shows clear signs of guilt."

Rachel's stomach twisted, but she remained composed. "Your Honor, the defendant has a documented history of dissociative episodes. We know that she has been under extreme stress, and we have expert psychological testimony that supports the idea that Emily's actions may have been the result of a psychological break, not premeditated murder."

Reid scoffed. "Your Honor, this is a textbook defence strategy—playing the mental illness card to escape responsibility. It's an insult to the victim's family."

Rachel's hands clenched at her sides, but she kept her gaze steady. She wasn't about to let Reid control the narrative. "This is not a 'card' we're playing, Mr. Reid. It's a fact."

The judge raised his hand, silencing them both. "I will review the arguments and make my decision. Court is adjourned."

As the session ended and the crowd began to file out, Rachel couldn't help but feel the weight of the world on her shoulders. The pressure was suffocating. She wasn't just defending Emily anymore. She was fighting a battle that went beyond the courtroom.

But she couldn't give up now. Not when they were so close to the truth.

And Rachel was determined to see it through to the end—no matter the cost.

Chapter 9: The Memory Trap

The sterile scent of antiseptic and the hum of fluorescent lights were familiar to Rachel as she entered Eli Warren's office. The walls were lined with bookshelves filled with medical journals, texts on psychiatry, and old leather-bound books whose pages had yellowed with age. Eli's office always had an air of quiet, professional restraint, but today, there was a palpable tension in the air.

Rachel glanced at the door leading into the adjacent therapy room, her stomach turning with a knot of worry. She wasn't sure what she expected—hope, maybe? Or perhaps dread, knowing the fragile state Emily was in. She had been with Eli for several sessions now, and Rachel had witnessed the toll the process was taking on her client. Each time Emily spoke of her past, it was as if she was unravelling, thread by thread.

But today, Rachel knew something would shift. The two of them had discussed this for weeks. Hypnosis. A last-ditch effort to unlock memories buried deep within Emily's subconscious. Eli believed it was the only way forward. It wasn't just a therapeutic technique—it was their best hope of proving Emily wasn't just a cold-blooded killer. She was a victim of something far more insidious.

As she walked into the room, she found Emily sitting in a comfortable chair, her hands folded neatly in her lap. Her face was pale, her eyes hollow from the strain of the last few weeks. She looked up as Rachel entered, offering her a weak smile.

"Are you okay?" Rachel asked softly, trying to keep her voice neutral.

Emily nodded but didn't speak. It was as if she were retreating into herself, a woman constantly on the edge of some breaking point she couldn't control. Rachel sat down across from her, noticing the way her hands twitched, the subtle fidgeting that spoke volumes about her inner turmoil.

Eli was sitting at his desk, looking over his notes. He was a tall man with sharp features, his salt-and-pepper hair only adding to his sense of authority. He was a man of reason, always calm, always collected. But even he couldn't hide the worry in his eyes when he looked at Emily.

"It's time," Eli said, his voice steady. He'd been using this calm tone with Emily for days, reassuring her when she faltered. He leaned back in his chair. "Emily, I need you to trust me. This isn't easy, but I promise we're going to work through this together. You're in control."

Emily swallowed hard, her breath quickening. "I don't know if I can," she whispered.

Rachel reached over and took her hand. "You don't have to do it alone," she said softly. "We're here with you."

Eli nodded. "When you're ready, Emily, I'll guide you through it. Just let go. Let your mind take you where it wants to go. We'll be right here."

Rachel held her breath, watching as Emily closed her eyes, trying to calm herself. Eli's voice was a steady presence as he began the hypnosis process, his words flowing like a gentle current, guiding Emily deeper and deeper into her mind.

At first, Emily's breathing slowed. Her body relaxed, her muscles unwinding under the weight of the technique. Rachel could see the subtle shift—the tension in Emily's posture melting away as she descended into a state of deep relaxation. But then, something in the air seemed to change, and Rachel noticed a flicker of unease pass across Eli's face.

"Emily," Eli's voice was soft but firm. "I want you to focus on your earliest memory. Let it come to you. Let it take shape."

For a moment, there was silence. And then Emily's voice broke through, quiet and distant.

"I... I remember... My mom. She used to yell at me all the time. It was... it was always about something I did wrong."

Eli's eyes narrowed slightly, but he kept his voice neutral. "That's good. Keep going, Emily. Tell me more."

The words that followed were disjointed at first. Fragments of memories, jumbled and incomplete, began to form in Emily's mind. The sounds of shouting. The smell of something burning in the kitchen. Her mother's face twisted in anger. But then, it was as though something snapped, and Emily's words became more erratic.

"I didn't mean to. I just wanted to help... She... she hit me. I didn't know what I did wrong. She kept hitting me... I tried to hide, but... she found me."

Rachel's heart clenched, and she felt the cold weight of dread settle over her. The room felt smaller, like the walls were closing in. She glanced at Eli, whose face had gone pale. He kept his voice calm, but Rachel could see the effort it took to maintain his composure.

"Emily, it's okay," Eli said softly. "You're safe now. No one is going to hurt you."

But Emily didn't seem to hear him. Her breathing quickened, and her voice grew more frantic. "She... she... I can't breathe! I can't—!"

Suddenly, Emily's body tensed violently, her hands gripping the arms of the chair as if she were trying to fight something invisible. A soft cry of terror escaped her lips, and Rachel could see the terror in her eyes even though they were closed.

Rachel shot to her feet, her heart racing. "What's happening to her?" she demanded, her voice trembling.

Eli was already moving toward Emily, placing his hand gently on her shoulder. "She's reliving something," he explained. "It's a memory that's been locked away for a long time. Let me help her."

Rachel watched in silent panic as Eli spoke calmly to Emily, guiding her through the waves of fear and disorientation. She could feel the tension in the room, the silent struggle between Emily's past and her present.

Minutes seemed to stretch on for an eternity. But finally, Emily's grip on the chair loosened, and her body relaxed again. Her breathing slowed, but her face remained strained, as though she were caught in the grip of something she couldn't escape.

"Emily?" Eli's voice was a whisper now, coaxing her back to reality. "I need you to come back. Slowly."

Emily's eyes fluttered open, and for a moment, she seemed lost—like a child who had wandered too far from home. Rachel moved closer, her hand hovering near Emily's, not quite touching her.

"Do you remember what happened?" Eli asked gently.

Emily blinked several times, her eyes unfocused. "I... I remember..." Her voice trailed off as she struggled to make sense of the images that had flooded her mind. "I don't know what happened. It's all mixed up."

Eli gave her a moment before speaking again, his voice steady but with an edge of concern. "What you remembered, Emily... it's important. We need to work through it, but you need to trust us. You're not alone."

Emily stared at him for a long time, her eyes full of confusion and fear. Finally, she nodded, though the effort seemed to cost her. "I don't know if I can handle this," she whispered, her voice barely audible.

Rachel knelt down beside her, her hand resting on Emily's arm. "You don't have to handle it all at once. You just need to take it one step at a time. We're here to help."

Eli took a step back, giving them space. His eyes met Rachel's—there was a knowing look in them, an understanding of the fragile balance they were now navigating. Emily's memory had just cracked open, revealing a hidden world of pain. But they weren't done yet. There was more to uncover, more that Emily would have to face. And with every revelation, the risk of unravelling Emily's fragile psyche grew greater.

"I can't promise it'll be easy," Eli said quietly. "But this is the breakthrough we've been waiting for."

Rachel nodded, but the unease in her chest only deepened. Emily had remembered something—something dark, something traumatic. But the question now was whether they could untangle the web of memories before it consumed Emily completely.

As they left Eli's office, Rachel couldn't shake the feeling that they had just stepped into something far darker than they could have imagined. A memory trap, where each answer only led to more questions, and every truth came at the cost of Emily's sanity.

And yet, Rachel couldn't stop herself from believing that this was the only way forward. For Emily's sake, she had to keep digging. No matter how painful the truth was.

Chapter 10: The Similar Case

Rachel sat alone in her office late that evening, the flickering glow of her laptop casting long shadows across the walls. The weight of the past few weeks was settling in her bones, each revelation about Emily's past adding another layer of heaviness to the case. She had never felt this mixture of urgency and unease before—not just as a lawyer, but as a person responsible for guiding a vulnerable soul through a trial that could change her life forever.

The case was already strange enough—a woman with a deeply fractured psyche, accused of a brutal murder she had no clear memory of. But now, as Rachel pored over police reports, court records, and a list of old newspaper clippings, something more sinister was emerging, something that sent a chill through her.

She had spent hours digging through every scrap of information she could find about Emily's life, especially her early years. It was painstaking work, a scavenger hunt through birth records, old therapy notes, and scattered documents. But then, as if it were waiting for her, she stumbled across it.

An unsolved case from years ago. A childhood friend. A brutal, unsolved murder.

The details were sparse, but familiar. The victim's name was Maria Ramos, and she had been a friend of Emily's in her youth, living just a few streets away from her family home. The police report Rachel managed to pull up listed it as an open investigation, but with no suspects or leads, it had faded into obscurity over the years. Maria had been found lifeless in the backyard of her own home, the scene gruesome, her small frame battered.

And the strangest part—the most disturbing detail of all—was that Maria's body had been positioned in a way that mirrored the scene Rachel had seen in the photographs of Emily's husband's death. It was as if some ghastly echo of Maria's death had repeated itself years later, with Emily's husband as the victim this time. The same horror, come back to haunt a different time, a different life.

Rachel's mind raced as she pieced together the fragments. It was a chilling revelation, one that unsettled her to her core. Emily's dissociative episodes weren't just isolated traumas. They seemed to be tethered to these darker memories, memories that had slumbered under layers of repression for years. Memories that Rachel now suspected might hold the key to understanding the truth behind her husband's murder.

She picked up her phone and dialled Eli's number, tapping her foot anxiously as she waited for him to answer. When he picked up, his voice was muffled with sleep.

"Rachel? Do you have any idea what time it is?"

"Sorry, Eli, but I think I've found something," she said quickly, her tone sharp. "This can't wait."

"Alright, I'm listening," he replied, fully awake now.

Rachel took a deep breath, her fingers tracing the edges of the old newspaper article in front of her. "I found a report on a murder from Emily's childhood. A girl named Maria Ramos. She was found dead in her backyard. And Eli, the way her body was found...it's eerily similar to what happened with Emily's husband."

There was a long pause on the other end, and Rachel could imagine Eli sitting up, his mind racing to catch up with her discovery.

"You're saying Emily might have witnessed a murder when she was young?" he asked slowly, his voice filled with disbelief.

"It's possible," Rachel said, her voice barely above a whisper. "But it's more than that. The parallels are too strong to ignore. This girl, Maria...she was Emily's friend. And if Emily's dissociative episodes were triggered by trauma, this could be a piece of the puzzle. Something she witnessed, something she never processed."

Eli was silent for a moment before he replied, his tone grave. "Rachel, do you realize what this could mean? If Emily witnessed a murder and her mind repressed it, then..."

"Then she might be repeating it," Rachel finished for him. The realization hit her with a force that left her momentarily speechless. "But not consciously. What if this trauma is manifesting itself in ways she can't control? This might not just be about her husband's murder—it could be a pattern."

"A pattern," Eli echoed. "One that's rooted in her childhood and resurfaced now. Rachel, this is dangerous territory. If we go down this path, it could unravel her completely."

Rachel closed her eyes, steeling herself against the doubt creeping in. "Eli, I know it's risky. But what if this is the answer? What if everything she's experienced, every blackout, every episode, is a piece of this buried truth?"

Eli sighed. "Alright. But if we're going to confront this, we need to proceed carefully. Emily's psyche is already fragile."

Rachel leaned back in her chair, her mind churning with the possibilities. She wasn't sure where this discovery would lead, but she knew one thing: there was no turning back.

The next morning, Rachel met Eli at his office. Emily was seated across from them, looking fragile yet determined. Her eyes darted between the two of them, sensing that something significant was about to unfold.

"Emily," Rachel began gently, "we found something from your past. Something about a friend you had when you were young—a girl named Maria Ramos."

Emily's face went blank, and for a moment, Rachel feared she'd shut down entirely. But then Emily's eyes flickered, a spark of recognition passing through them. She opened her mouth to speak, but the words seemed to catch in her throat.

"Maria…" she whispered, her voice distant. "She…she was my friend."

Rachel nodded; her voice soft. "Can you tell us about her?"

Emily hesitated; her gaze fixed on a spot somewhere far away. "We used to play together. I remember…we'd run through the park, climb trees. But one day…"

Her voice trailed off, her brow furrowing as she struggled to reach for a memory just out of grasp.

"One day, Maria went missing," Emily continued, her voice barely above a whisper. "And then…she was gone. I remember my mom telling me she had to move away. That I wouldn't see her again."

Eli leaned forward, his voice calm. "Emily, do you remember what happened to Maria? Anything about that day?"

Emily's breathing grew shallow, her body tensing as flashes of memory surfaced. "I don't…I don't know. I just remember feeling scared. So, so scared. But I don't know why."

Rachel exchanged a glance with Eli. They were peeling back the layers of Emily's past, one painful memory at a time, but the pieces weren't fitting together just yet. Emily's mind was guarding something, hiding it even from herself.

"Emily," Rachel pressed gently, "there's something important you need to know. Maria didn't move away. She was found dead, in her backyard.

And the way she...the way she died was...similar to what happened with your husband."

Emily's face went pale, her body recoiling as if she'd been slapped. Her hands gripped the armrests of her chair, her knuckles turning white. "No," she murmured, shaking her head. "That's not...that can't be true."

Rachel reached out, placing a comforting hand on Emily's arm. "I know this is hard to hear. But if this memory—if what happened to Maria—is connected to what happened to your husband, we need to understand it."

Eli leaned closer; his voice soft but unyielding. "Emily, we believe you may have repressed memories of that time. Memories that could be affecting you now. I want to help you access them, but only if you're ready."

Emily stared at them both, her eyes wide and filled with terror. For a long moment, she didn't move, her gaze lost in some distant place neither Rachel nor Eli could reach. But then, slowly, she nodded, her voice a whisper.

"I want to remember," she said, her voice trembling. "I need to know."

As they began the hypnosis session, Rachel's heart pounded. She felt the weight of every question, every doubt, resting on Emily's fragile shoulders. She watched as Eli guided her client back to that dark place, coaxing her gently toward the memories she had hidden away for so long.

Emily's breathing slowed, her body relaxing as she slipped into a trance. And then, as if dredged up from the depths of her mind, fragments of memory began to surface. The sound of laughter, a girl's voice, the feel of the rough bark of a tree under her hands. And then, darkness—a cold, suffocating fear that wrapped around her like a shroud.

"I was there," Emily murmured, her voice barely audible. "I was with her...with Maria...and..."

Her voice caught, and a single tear rolled down her cheek. "There was someone else. Watching us. I don't know who...but he was...waiting."

Rachel's heart raced as she listened, every word bringing them closer to a truth that was both terrifying and essential. Emily was piecing it together, step by painful step. But as she spoke, as she relived that haunting day, Rachel realized that the truth they were unearthing might be darker than anything she'd ever imagined.

Emily's whispered words lingered in the air, a fragile bridge to a buried truth.

"Maria...she didn't fall. He...he hurt her. And I just...I ran."

Chapter 11: Trial Preparations

The courtroom was as sterile as Rachel had expected, its gleaming wood surfaces and towering shelves lined with dusty legal volumes evoking an air of cold authority. Despite years in this field, Rachel felt a knot tightening in her stomach—a warning of the high stakes this case carried.

As Rachel arranged her files at the defence table, she glanced over at Emily, who sat with her shoulders hunched, eyes cast downward. There was something different about Emily now, a deepening in her gaze that revealed a new layer of fear. The recent revelations about Maria, and the memories of that fateful day, had left her raw and vulnerable. They had brought Emily closer to the truth, but at a cost neither of them had fully anticipated.

Rachel took a seat beside her, leaning in with a reassuring smile. "Emily, I know this is overwhelming, but we're prepared. I've gone over every possible angle for your defence. We're going to argue that this is a case of insanity, rooted in a lifetime of untreated trauma. You're not alone in this."

Emily's hands were clasped so tightly that her knuckles were white. She took a shaky breath, looking up at Rachel with a tortured expression. "What if...what if they're right about me? What if I really did it?"

Rachel squeezed her shoulder. "Emily, listen to me. The fact that you're even asking that question proves that you're not a killer. We're going to fight this. I'll do everything in my power to make sure the jury understands the truth."

But even as she spoke, Rachel felt the pressure closing in. She had spent countless hours researching, building a case around Emily's dissociative identity disorder and her trauma-induced episodes. Yet the prosecutor, a seasoned attorney with a reputation for crushing defences, was ready to counter every point. Rachel had seen his strategies before: he would leverage the sympathy of the jury, painting Emily as not a victim, but a manipulative threat who exploited her mental health as an excuse for violence.

She couldn't deny that the prosecutor's argument was compelling. The case had garnered significant media attention, and public sentiment had already turned against Emily. Headlines painted her as a "cold-blooded wife," the media capitalizing on every lurid detail and implying guilt before a verdict had even been reached.

That afternoon, Rachel and Eli huddled in her office, finalizing their strategy. Stacks of files and evidence covered every inch of her desk. Eli was deep in thought, flipping through a binder filled with notes from his sessions with Emily.

"This is going to be a battle, Rachel," he murmured. "The prosecutor's approach is brutal, and he's going to paint Emily as dangerously unstable."

Rachel nodded. "That's why we need to emphasize that Emily's actions—if she even did commit them—weren't under her conscious control. Her history of dissociation, her traumatic childhood, and her diagnosis of DID—these factors have to be at the centre of our argument."

Eli looked at her, his expression wary. "Rachel, we need to be careful. Emily's trauma runs so deep, and pushing her to remember things she's spent years burying…it's risky. We could be reopening wounds that will take years to heal."

"I know, Eli. But she deserves a fair defence. And the truth deserves to come out."

Eli sighed, rubbing his temples. "Just know that if we go down this road, we're not just defending Emily in a courtroom. We're digging into something that's bound to unsettle her."

Rachel was silent, contemplating his words. There was no other way. The only chance they had was to lay bare every detail, every dark memory, to show the jury that Emily was as much a victim as her late husband.

They worked late into the night, preparing for the uphill battle that awaited them. Eli would testify on Emily's behalf, detailing her dissociative identity disorder and its impact on her actions. Rachel would present evidence of Emily's history of blackouts and dissociative episodes, framing them as responses to trauma, beyond her conscious control.

But as the night dragged on, Rachel couldn't shake the feeling that there was still more lurking beneath the surface of Emily's memories, secrets that hadn't yet been uncovered.

The following morning, Emily sat across from Rachel in the office, listening as Rachel outlined the strategy for her testimony. Her face was pale, her eyes filled with doubt.

"So…you're going to tell them I'm insane?" Emily's voice was barely a whisper.

Rachel placed a hand on hers. "Not insane. We're telling them that you've been through severe trauma, trauma that you were too young to process. Your mind found ways to protect you from it, but that's caused you to have dissociative episodes."

Emily shook her head, her voice trembling. "But…what if that's just an excuse? What if I really am just…just violent?"

"No," Rachel said firmly, her eyes locked on Emily's. "That's not who you are. You've been shaped by experiences you couldn't control. This isn't about guilt or innocence in the traditional sense. It's about understanding the complex ways trauma affects a person's mind."

Emily nodded, though she still looked unsure. Rachel could tell that Emily was wrestling with guilt and doubt, her self-image battered by weeks of scrutiny and the horror of her husband's murder.

Rachel leaned in; her voice gentle but steady. "Emily, the prosecutor is going to try to portray you as manipulative, as someone who used mental illness as a cover for violent behaviour. But we're going to show the truth. I need you to trust me, and to trust yourself."

Emily swallowed hard, her eyes glistening. "I…I'll try."

On the day of the pre-trial motions, Rachel walked into the courtroom, her spine straight, her expression focused. Eli sat beside her, scanning the courtroom with a look of quiet determination. Across the aisle, the prosecutor was hunched over a file, occasionally glancing up at Emily with a gaze that made her shift uncomfortably.

As the prosecutor began his opening remarks, Rachel felt the tension in the room rise. He launched into a monologue about the duty of the court to protect society from "dangerous individuals" who used "so-called mental illness" as a way to escape justice. He emphasized Emily's "carefully orchestrated manipulation," framing her as a cold and calculating woman who saw herself as above the law.

Rachel clenched her fists, biting back her frustration. She knew that this was only the beginning, that his arguments would become even more cutting as the trial progressed. But she also knew that she had a responsibility to show the other side of Emily's story, the side that the public—and even the jury—had yet to see.

When it was her turn to speak, Rachel took a deep breath, steadying her voice. "Ladies and gentlemen of the jury, my client, Emily Grant, is not the monster she's been portrayed to be. What we have here is a tragedy, a case of unimaginable pain and suffering. Emily's life has been marred by trauma from a young age, trauma that led to her dissociative episodes. She's not a danger to society—she's a victim of circumstances beyond her control."

She glanced at Emily, who sat with her hands clasped tightly in her lap, her head bowed. Rachel continued, "Our goal is not to excuse her actions, but to provide context, to help you understand the depth of her suffering and the impact it has had on her mind. We ask only that you look at her not as a criminal, but as a human being struggling to make sense of a world that has dealt her unimaginable hardship."

As she finished, Rachel saw a flicker of empathy in the faces of a few jurors. It was a small victory, but it was a start.

After the motions concluded, Rachel and Eli retreated to her office to review the arguments they would present at trial. Rachel could feel the strain in the air; they both knew this case would test their limits.

Eli broke the silence. "Rachel, I need you to be prepared for the fact that this trial is going to get ugly. The prosecutor will do everything he can to dismantle our defence, to cast doubt on Emily's trauma and dissociation."

Rachel nodded, her jaw set. "I know, Eli. But we're going to stand firm. Emily deserves to have her story heard, and I won't let anyone strip her of her humanity."

Eli looked at her with a mix of respect and concern. "You're doing something brave, Rachel. But just be careful not to let this case consume you. You're carrying a lot on your shoulders."

Rachel managed a faint smile. "It's my job to carry it. And for Emily's sake, I'm willing to bear every ounce of it."

As they reviewed their notes one final time, Rachel felt the weight of the trial bearing down on her. She knew that the days ahead would be gruelling, each step forward fraught with challenges. But she also knew that she couldn't back down—not now, not ever.

Emily's life was in her hands, and she was ready to fight with everything she had.

Chapter 12: The First Day in Court

The courtroom was packed. Reporters lined the back wall, fingers poised over their laptops, ready to broadcast every move, every word, every flicker of emotion on Emily's face. The gallery held a mix of onlookers, some sympathetic, others with hardened faces that spoke of judgment before evidence had even been presented. The air was thick with anticipation as the bailiff called the court to order.

Rachel took a deep breath, glancing over at Emily, who sat beside her. Emily's face was unreadable, her eyes fixed on a point in the distance, almost as if she were anywhere but here. Rachel placed a reassuring hand on her shoulder, but Emily didn't react, her body still and tense.

"All rise," the bailiff intoned, and Judge Morrison entered, settling at his bench with a stern gaze sweeping the room.

"Let's begin," he said, nodding toward the prosecutor, who stood up, smoothing his already impeccable suit. Charles Hathaway was a veteran prosecutor, a man known for his unflinching style and sharp arguments. His gaze was cold as he turned toward the jury, his tone steady and cutting.

"Ladies and gentlemen of the jury," Hathaway began, "we're here today to bring justice to a man who lost his life in the prime of his years, his future stolen by the very person he trusted most." He walked deliberately toward the jury box, allowing his words to settle in. "This case is not about mental illness, or trauma, or excuses. It is about cold, calculated murder."

He gestured toward Emily, who sat motionless, her head slightly bowed. "Emily Grant, the defendant, didn't snap. She didn't have a psychotic break. No, she planned this. She waited for the right moment, the perfect moment, to take her husband's life in the most brutal fashion imaginable."

Rachel watched the jury, reading their expressions as they took in his words. Hathaway's voice was like a scalpel, slicing through the air with precision. He painted a picture of Emily that was both chilling and relentless: a woman who had used her vulnerability as a weapon, who had exploited her husband's trust only to betray him in the most unforgivable way. Rachel's stomach twisted as she sensed the weight of Hathaway's words seeping into the minds of the jurors.

Hathaway continued, his voice growing softer, almost conspiratorial. "The defence will ask you to look at her as a victim. They'll tell you stories of her past, of her struggles. They'll weave a tale meant to pull at your heartstrings. But I ask you to remember, as you sit here and listen, that the true victim in this case is not Emily Grant. It is her husband, a man who will never again breathe, never again laugh, never again live."

He paused, letting his words sink in before delivering his final line with chilling precision. "I intend to show you that Emily Grant is not the woman the defence will try to portray. She is a killer, and she must be held accountable."

As Hathaway returned to his seat, a murmur rippled through the courtroom. Rachel felt Emily shift beside her, a tremor passing through her hands as she gripped the edge of the table.

Rachel stood, her heart pounding, knowing this was her moment to reframe the narrative, to chip away at the stone Hathaway had cast around Emily.

"Ladies and gentlemen of the jury," she began, her voice warm but resolute, "what you just heard is one interpretation of the story—a story that is dark and terrifying, yes. But it is a story that's been crafted to strip Emily Grant of her humanity."

She looked each juror in the eye, holding their gaze, letting them see her own conviction. "What we have here is not a cold-blooded killer. What we have is a young woman who has been through unimaginable pain and trauma, a woman who has suffered since childhood and has been let down by every safety net meant to protect her. Emily Grant's life has been a series of wounds, some of which have scarred so deeply that her mind has had to shield itself to survive."

Rachel's voice softened, taking on an almost maternal tone. "This case is not black and white, no matter how the prosecution wants to paint it. Emily has lived with a condition known as dissociative identity disorder, brought on by trauma that fractured her mind into pieces she could only keep hidden. This case is about understanding—not excusing, but understanding—a woman who has lived on the edge of her own mind for most of her life."

Rachel felt the room tense as she continued, her words a plea that resonated beyond logic, striking at something deeper. "I ask that you consider not just the evidence, but the context. Consider the humanity of the woman sitting here before you, a woman who has lived a life shaped by circumstances beyond her control. I ask you to look at Emily as a person—a fragile, broken person who needs help, not condemnation."

When Rachel sat down, she could feel the energy in the room had shifted, if only slightly. The jury looked conflicted, some glancing back at Emily with a new glimmer of empathy. Beside her, Emily's breathing was shallow, her face pale as she clung to Rachel's words as if they were a lifeline.

As the first witness took the stand—a police officer who had been present during Emily's arrest—Rachel noticed Emily's demeanour begin to shift. At first, she sat tense but composed, listening carefully to each word. But as the officer described the scene—the blood, Emily's disoriented state, her muttering of words that made little sense—Emily's gaze turned vacant, her shoulders curling inward as if she were shrinking from an invisible force.

Rachel leaned in, whispering gently, "Emily, stay with me. Focus on my voice."

But Emily's eyes were glazed, her breathing shallow. Rachel recognized the signs—a dissociative episode was creeping over her, the courtroom's intensity and the officer's vivid words pushing her to the edge.

The officer recounted the moment he found her, describing her as "lost" and "disturbing," his words laced with suspicion. Emily's expression shifted, her gaze flickering with something dark, almost unfamiliar. Rachel saw the muscles in her face tense, her hands clenching, and realized that the jury was watching her closely, taking in every nuance of her reaction.

Rachel placed a hand over Emily's, grounding her, her own pulse racing as she whispered, "Emily, focus. It's just words. They can't hurt you."

Emily blinked, her expression softening, her breathing slowing as she let herself be anchored by Rachel's touch. But Rachel knew the jury had seen enough to plant seeds of doubt—seeds Hathaway would undoubtedly nurture when he cross-examined her.

During the lunch recess, Rachel and Eli retreated to a quiet corner of the courthouse cafeteria. Eli was visibly tense, stirring his coffee absentmindedly as he glanced toward the courtroom doors.

"She's on edge, Rachel. Her mind is fraying under the pressure. We have to be careful; if she loses control in there, Hathaway will capitalize on it."

Rachel nodded, exhaling slowly. "I know. It's like walking a tightrope. I've done everything I can to prepare her, but these episodes…they're unpredictable. It's why I insisted on grounding exercises, but even that's not enough sometimes."

Eli leaned forward; his voice low. "If we can't manage her dissociation during trial, the jury is going to see exactly what Hathaway wants them to see: a woman capable of snapping, of losing herself in a rage. It's a thin line between sympathy and fear."

"I can't give up on her, Eli. Not when we're this close to getting the truth out." Rachel's voice was fierce, a reflection of the conviction that had driven her this far.

Eli's gaze softened. "I know, Rachel. But we have to be realistic. We can't let our dedication blind us to the danger here."

Rachel clenched her jaw, glancing toward the court doors. "No matter how difficult it is, Emily deserves a chance to be heard. I won't let Hathaway silence her or twist her suffering into something ugly."

As they walked back to the courtroom, Rachel's resolve hardened. She would fight for Emily, against every ounce of Hathaway's fierce strategy, against the odds stacked against them. For Emily, this was not just a trial; it was a battle for her very identity, a chance to reclaim the fragments of herself scattered by years of trauma.

As the day progressed, the court heard from several more witnesses, each testimony chipping away at Emily's defence. But through it all, Rachel stood firm, countering each blow with meticulous questions and unwavering confidence.

When the court finally adjourned for the day, Rachel looked over at Emily, whose shoulders sagged under the weight of exhaustion. For a moment, she saw the flicker of a little girl lost in a storm of memories, haunted by visions she couldn't control.

Rachel placed a hand on her shoulder, guiding her out of the courtroom, whispering, "We're going to get through this, Emily. One day at a time."

Emily looked up at her, a faint spark of hope in her weary eyes. For the first time, there was a trace of belief there—a fragile but undeniable belief that perhaps, just perhaps, she was not alone in this fight.

Chapter 13: An Unseen Manipulator

Eli sat at his desk; files spread out before him in a meticulous order. He leaned back, rubbing his temples, trying to piece together what had been gnawing at the edge of his mind since they'd begun this case. The deeper he delved into the life of Emily's husband, Patrick Grant, the more certain inconsistencies emerged—details that hinted he might not have been the loving husband everyone assumed.

After their intense day in court, Eli couldn't shake the feeling that there was something far more sinister in Patrick's role in Emily's life. He'd combed through Patrick's psychological records, his personal journals, and finally, accounts from people who had known him. And what he was finding was disturbing.

It was nearly midnight when his phone buzzed with a message from Rachel.

"Any updates?"

Eli stared at the screen before typing back.

"I think I've found something. We need to talk in person."

The following morning, Eli and Rachel met at a small café near the courthouse. Rachel arrived with a look of weary determination, clearly pushed to her limits but still determined to fight. Eli motioned for her to sit, his expression grave.

"What did you find?" Rachel asked, not even waiting to order a coffee. The urgency in her voice was palpable.

Eli leaned in, lowering his voice. "There are patterns in Patrick's background, Rachel. Things that don't add up." He pulled a file from his bag and laid it open between them. "It seems that Patrick may have known about Emily's mental health struggles long before she ever confided in him."

Rachel frowned, confused. "But Emily told us she didn't open up to him about her dissociative episodes until months after they were married."

Eli nodded. "That's what she believes. But Patrick had a history of relationships with women who had mental health issues. In fact, there are whispers of previous relationships where he had power over vulnerable women, manipulating them under the guise of 'helping' them."

Rachel's eyes widened as she leaned closer. "Are you saying Patrick might have deliberately exploited Emily's condition?"

Eli's jaw tightened. "It's possible. I've spoken with an old colleague of his—a psychiatrist who worked with Patrick at a university clinic years ago. This colleague recalled an incident where Patrick showed an almost unhealthy curiosity about dissociative disorders. He even conducted research on people who had a history of trauma."

Rachel's mind raced. "So…Patrick could have known exactly what he was doing when he married Emily."

Eli nodded grimly. "And if he knew about her dissociative identity disorder before she even confided in him, he may have carefully orchestrated situations to bring out her episodes. If he could trigger her dissociation at will, he'd be in complete control over her memories, her reality, her perception of their relationship."

Rachel shuddered at the thought. "He was manipulating her all along, wasn't he?"

Eli glanced around the café, making sure no one was listening, and continued in a low tone. "There's more. I looked through Emily's medical records. There were periods where she experienced sudden and severe anxiety attacks, episodes of paranoia that she thought were completely random. But these attacks happened during specific times—times that align suspiciously well with when Patrick would disappear on business trips or be out of touch."

"So, he'd leave, knowing she'd spiral," Rachel murmured, her stomach churning. "And she'd be alone, suffering, with no one to turn to but him."

Later that day, Rachel and Eli returned to their office, armed with Patrick's records and a new sense of purpose. They combed through the documents, piecing together a profile of Patrick that painted him as a master manipulator, a man skilled at exploiting the vulnerabilities of those around him.

And then they found something that sent chills down Rachel's spine—a hidden clause in Patrick's life insurance policy, listing Emily as the sole beneficiary. The policy had been updated only months before his death, almost as if Patrick had set this all in motion, knowing that his wife's fractured mind would be an easy scapegoat.

"These changes everything," Rachel whispered, staring at the paper in her hands. "Patrick wasn't just a victim—he was an architect in his own demise. He set her up."

Eli ran a hand over his face, the weight of the discovery settling over him. "If we can prove that he manipulated her, that he knew about her condition and used it against her, it could shift the entire case. It might even lead to a dismissal if we can show she was pushed to a psychological breaking point."

Rachel's mind raced through the possibilities. The evidence wasn't definitive, but it opened doors—doors they could push on until something gave way.

The next day in court, Rachel couldn't shake the new image of Patrick she now held in her mind. As she watched the jury's faces, she felt an odd sense of validation, knowing she was one step closer to unveiling the truth.

Emily took the stand, visibly shaken but with a newfound resolve in her eyes. Rachel approached her, her voice soft but commanding.

"Emily, I know this is difficult, but I want to ask you some questions about your husband," Rachel began, careful to keep her tone gentle.

Emily's hands trembled as she clutched the edge of the witness stand. "Okay," she murmured, her voice barely above a whisper.

Rachel moved closer; her gaze sympathetic but focused. "Did Patrick ever make you feel like your episodes were something to be ashamed of?"

Emily's eyes darted nervously, as if the words themselves were laced with danger. "Yes... he would tell me that my episodes were embarrassing, that they made me weak. He said that if people knew, they'd think I was crazy."

Rachel nodded. "And did he ever encourage you to seek help for your episodes, or did he discourage it?"

Emily hesitated, her brow furrowing as memories surfaced. "At first, he said he wanted to help me, that he could help me better than any doctor could. But then... he would use my episodes against me. If I had a blackout, he'd tell me things I did—things I didn't remember doing—and I'd feel horrible."

Rachel's voice softened even further. "Did you ever have the feeling that he was... guiding you, or controlling how you felt about yourself?"

Emily's eyes filled with tears as she nodded. "Yes. Sometimes, I didn't know what was real anymore. He'd say things like, 'You're too fragile for the world,' or 'You need me to protect you.' It was like… he wanted me to believe I couldn't survive without him."

Rachel glanced toward the jury, seeing them lean in, listening intently. She turned back to Emily, her voice a thread of steel. "Emily, did Patrick ever tell you about his interest in dissociative identity disorder?"

Emily's face paled, and she shook her head slowly. "No… he never mentioned it. But now that I think about it… he seemed to know a lot about my episodes. More than I did."

The prosecutor rose, clearly agitated. "Objection, Your Honor. This is speculation."

Judge Morrison looked at Rachel, who held up her hands in acquiescence. "Withdrawn," she said, though the damage was done. The jury had heard it, and the seed of doubt had been planted.

That evening, Rachel and Eli sat in her office; the weight of the day's testimony heavy between them.

"That was powerful, Rachel," Eli said, his voice quiet but admiring. "You're exposing Patrick's manipulation, bit by bit."

Rachel exhaled, rubbing her temples. "It's risky, but it's the only way. If the jury can see Patrick as a hidden manipulator, they might start to question everything. Including whether Emily had control over her actions."

Eli nodded thoughtfully. "You're reshaping the entire narrative. It's not Emily as the aggressor—it's her as the pawn in a game she never knew she was playing."

Rachel's gaze drifted to the window, her mind whirling with possibilities. "I just need to make them see it. If they can see that Patrick engineered this whole thing, even if only to push her to the brink, it could be enough. It has to be enough."

Eli leaned back; his face serious. "And what if they don't see it?"

Rachel's expression hardened, a fierce determination settling over her. "Then we keep fighting. Because I'm not giving up on her—not until every hidden truth is dragged into the light."

Eli gave a small nod, respect evident in his eyes. They were up against a system that rarely sided with the vulnerable, a system that often chose the simplest answer. But Rachel had found her anchor, her purpose—and she would see it through, no matter the cost.

As they left the office that night, Rachel felt a renewed sense of resolve. She knew they were inching closer to the truth, uncovering secrets that Patrick had worked so hard to keep buried. The weight of it all was daunting, but with every revelation, she felt the scales tipping, one truth at a time.

Chapter 14: Expert Testimonies

The courtroom was electric with anticipation, buzzing with the murmurs of spectators and the shifting of seats as everyone settled in. This was the day the defence would put Dr. Eli Warren on the stand, and Rachel knew that how Eli presented his testimony could make or break their case. His explanation of dissociative identity disorder (DID) was essential to Emily's defence, yet she also knew that it would be a hard sell in a room full of people whose knowledge of mental health was shaped more by sensationalized headlines than scientific truth.

Rachel stole a glance at Eli, who sat a few rows away, his face calm and unreadable as ever. They'd spent hours preparing, going over every possible question, anticipating every twist that the prosecutor, Charles Wade, might use to discredit him. Eli was ready, but Rachel could see a faint tension in his shoulders as he waited to be called forward.

Finally, Judge Morrison nodded at Rachel. "The defence may proceed."

Rachel rose, her heels clicking sharply against the floor as she approached the witness stand. "The defence calls Dr. Eli Warren to the stand."

Eli stood, his movements smooth and confident as he made his way to the witness box. He took his oath, then sat down, adjusting his glasses and casting a quick look at Rachel. She gave him a small, reassuring nod before turning to face the jury.

"Dr. Warren, could you please explain to the court what dissociative identity disorder, or DID, entails?" Rachel began, her voice steady.

Eli leaned forward, addressing the jury with an approachable calm. "Dissociative identity disorder is a condition characterized by a fragmentation of identity. It's often a response to severe trauma, typically in early childhood. In simple terms, DID is a survival mechanism. When a person is exposed to prolonged trauma, especially when they're very young, their mind may split off different 'selves' to handle the pain and fear. These alternate identities, or 'alters,' often serve specific roles in the individual's life, helping them navigate situations that feel overwhelming or dangerous."

The jury leaned in, absorbing his words. Eli's tone was compassionate, free of the clinical detachment some might have expected. Rachel noted how some jurors appeared sympathetic, even intrigued, while others wore sceptical expressions, arms crossed or brows furrowed.

"And would you say that someone with DID has full control over these alternate identities?" Rachel continued.

"No, they don't," Eli answered firmly. "The nature of DID is that these identities operate independently, often without the person's conscious awareness. In cases like Emily's, an alter might take control to protect her from situations that trigger traumatic memories or feelings. It's as if one part of her mind steps forward to shield her from pain, but Emily herself may have no memory of what that identity does while in control."

Rachel nodded, moving to her next question. "So, Dr. Warren, in your expert opinion, could Emily Grant's DID have impacted her behaviour on the night of her husband's death?"

Eli met her gaze before answering, then looked toward the jury. "Yes. It's highly likely that one of Emily's alters emerged as a response to something traumatic that evening. And it's also likely that Emily has no memory of what happened during that time, given the dissociative nature of her condition."

Rachel offered a brief smile, then stepped aside. "Thank you, Dr. Warren. No further questions."

She returned to her seat, but the momentary relief faded as she watched Charles Wade rise, straightening his suit before approaching Eli. Wade's expression was one of calculated scepticism, and Rachel could sense the tension in the room mounting as he prepared to dissect Eli's testimony.

"Dr. Warren," Wade began, a slight smirk playing at his lips, "you claim that dissociative identity disorder is a response to trauma, is that correct?"

"Yes," Eli replied, his voice steady.

Wade nodded, as if considering this carefully. "And yet, you admit that DID is controversial, do you not? Many experts disagree on its legitimacy as a diagnosis."

Eli's jaw tightened subtly, but he held his composure. "There is some debate, yes, but DID is a recognized diagnosis in the DSM-5, the main diagnostic manual used by mental health professionals."

"But isn't it true," Wade pressed, "that DID have been popularized in books and movies, sometimes giving rise to so-called 'false memories or leading people to believe they have multiple personalities when they do not?"

Eli's voice remained calm, but there was a steeliness to his gaze as he met Wade's eyes. "While the media has sensationalized DID, that does not mean it isn't real. There's significant research supporting it as a legitimate condition. And the experiences of people with DID are complex and often misrepresented by those who lack a full understanding of the disorder."

Wade's mouth twisted slightly, as though unimpressed. "Is it possible that Emily Grant could be fabricating these symptoms?"

Eli paused, choosing his words carefully. "People with DID typically don't 'fabricate' their symptoms. The condition is often accompanied by amnesia or confusion, which would be difficult to fake. In my experience,

Emily's symptoms are consistent with someone who has experienced significant trauma and dissociates to protect herself."

Wade didn't miss a beat, turning to the jury as he continued his line of questioning. "You say she dissociates to 'protect herself.' But could that also be a convenient excuse to avoid responsibility for a crime?"

Eli's face remained neutral, but Rachel saw the flicker of frustration in his eyes. "DID is not an 'excuse.' It's a condition that complicates an individual's ability to process reality in the way most people do. Emily's actions, if they occurred during a dissociative episode, were likely outside her conscious control."

Wade leaned back; arms crossed. "So, what you're saying, Dr. Warren, is that Emily could have committed this crime without even realizing it. That she could be both innocent and guilty at the same time. Is that what you're proposing?"

The room went silent, everyone's eyes locked on Eli. He took a deep breath before responding, his voice calm and measured. "I'm saying that mental illness is complex, and the mind sometimes operates in ways that defy simple labels like 'innocent' or 'guilty.' Emily's condition means she experiences reality in fragments, and we must take that into account when assessing her actions."

The jury members exchanged glances, their faces reflecting a spectrum of reactions—from empathy to doubt. Wade, sensing a divide, seized the moment.

"Thank you, Dr. Warren. No further questions," he said, his tone clipped, as though he'd proven his point.

Eli stepped down from the stand, his expression calm but his shoulders tense. Rachel felt a pang of frustration; Wade had cast a shadow of doubt, and she could see it lingering on the faces of the jurors, each of them processing the implications of Eli's testimony. She'd hoped the jury would feel the depth of Emily's suffering, but Wade's performance had muddied the waters, blurring the line between psychological truth and convenient justification.

After court adjourned for the day, Rachel and Eli walked out of the courthouse together, their expressions sombre. The wind whipped around them, bringing a chill that matched Rachel's mood. She knew that today's testimony had shaken the jury's confidence, and she was struggling to think of a way to counter Wade's scepticism.

"You held up well, Eli," she said, attempting to sound reassuring.

Eli gave her a wry smile, though his eyes remained troubled. "Wade knows how to play to the jury's emotions. He's casting doubt, making them question if DID is just a label we use to avoid accountability."

Rachel clenched her jaw. "He's deliberately exploiting their lack of understanding about mental health. But we can't let him turn this into a battle of prejudice over empathy."

Eli's expression softened. "Rachel, we knew this wouldn't be easy. People don't like to see complexities in criminal cases—they want clear-cut answers, simple motives. But DID defies that. It makes people uncomfortable."

They walked in silence for a moment, each lost in their own thoughts.

"Tomorrow, I want to try a different approach," Rachel finally said. "If I can bring out Emily's vulnerability, maybe they'll see her as a victim of her circumstances, not just a potential perpetrator. We need to show them the human side of this—not just theories and symptoms."

Eli nodded; his confidence seemingly renewed. "I think you're right. This isn't just about presenting a diagnosis; it's about making them feel her pain, understand her struggle. We need to bring out the parts of Emily that are hidden beneath all those fragmented memories."

Rachel looked at him, a spark of hope igniting within her. "Then let's do it. Let's show them who Emily really is."

As they walked into the gathering dusk, Rachel felt the weight of their challenge, but she also felt a fierce resolve. She was fighting not only for Emily's life, but for a new understanding of justice—one that would consider the depths of the mind, the layers of trauma, and the complex boundaries between victim and perpetrator.

Chapter 15: A Desperate Discovery

The office was dimly lit, the sky outside already melting into the inky black of evening, but Rachel barely noticed the encroaching darkness. Papers were strewn across her desk, stacks and files and photographs arranged in clusters around her, creating a chaotic map of Emily's case. Every piece of evidence, every report, every tiny detail she'd gathered lay before her, yet something still felt missing.

She pushed a hand through her hair, frustration simmering beneath the surface. How many times had she combed through these files? And still, every path seemed to lead to the same, murky crossroads. If she couldn't find something solid, something that would get the jury to see the truth, all this work would have been in vain. Emily's life depended on uncovering that missing piece.

Just as she was about to call it a night, a knock sounded on her office door. She looked up to see her assistant, Claire, standing there with an odd expression.

"Rachel, this just arrived," Claire said, holding up a package. It was worn and faded, as though it had been handled by a dozen people on its way to her. Rachel took it, frowning as she looked it over. There was no return address, just her name scrawled in ink that was smudged and faint.

"Who brought this?" she asked, turning it over in her hands.

"Some courier. He said it was urgent," Claire replied, clearly unsettled.

Rachel set the package on her desk and opened it carefully, slipping her fingers beneath the edge of the tape. Inside, she found an old, weathered journal, its leather cover cracked and worn. Her heart thudded with a strange mix of dread and anticipation as she flipped open the first page. There, in unmistakable handwriting, was the name *Ian Grant*—Emily's late husband.

Rachel's pulse quickened as she turned the pages, her eyes skimming over handwritten notes, entries written in a mix of calm detachment and eerie, obsessive detail. The dates on each entry went back months, some of them even years, cataloguing what appeared to be Ian's meticulous observations of Emily's behaviour.

With a growing sense of unease, Rachel began to read.

January 7th: Noticed Emily has become more forgetful. She lost track of a full day last week and couldn't recall where she'd been. She seemed frightened when I asked her about it, but I reassured her it was nothing to worry about. I'll monitor this further.

February 14th: Emily entered one of her "states" again, though this time it lasted longer. She didn't recognize me at first, looked right through me as if I were a stranger. I used the opportunity to test her reactions, asking questions about her past. She seemed distant, detached, as if she were only half there.

March 3rd: Progress. I've been subtly creating situations that might trigger her episodes. It's fascinating how predictable her shifts are when given the right cues. I'm curious if these episodes are as involuntary as she claims, or if part of her is choosing to escape. Will escalate tests.

Rachel's hand trembled as she turned the page, her stomach churning with every new entry. It was worse than she'd feared. This wasn't just documentation; it was manipulation. Ian hadn't been an innocent bystander, swept up in his wife's complex struggles. He'd been orchestrating her mental breakdown, pushing her toward the very edge where reality blurred, and she lost herself.

She continued to read, her breath shallow.

April 19th: Emily had another blackout. This one was intense. I provoked her by bringing up her father's death, which usually unsettles her. She grew confused, angry—then blank. For a few minutes, she wasn't Emily. She was... something else. Someone else. She even changed her tone, her posture. I wonder how far I can push her before she breaks.

Rachel swallowed hard, bile rising in her throat. This was evidence of outright abuse. Ian had preyed on her mental health, had gone out of his way to fracture her psyche further, deliberately driving her into dissociative episodes for his own twisted curiosity. He hadn't loved her. He'd used her as an experiment.

The more she read, the clearer it became. Ian had carefully crafted Emily's psychological torment, tailoring scenarios that would trigger her dissociation. He'd built a world for her out of fear and uncertainty, manipulating her past traumas like an artist with a palette of pain and doubt.

Rachel's heart raced with a mixture of horror and hope. This was the missing piece. This journal was proof that Emily had been a victim, not just of her own mind but of someone else's cruelty. This could change everything.

But even as she felt the triumph building, a new dread crept in. The entries grew darker, Ian's tone shifting from detached curiosity to something more menacing.

June 2nd: She's beginning to suspect something. I caught her looking at me oddly today, as if she could see right through my questions, my prompts. I'll have to be more careful, but I need to keep pushing. I'm close—so close to seeing what's hidden beneath. But there's a risk now. She's unpredictable when she switches. Perhaps I've gone too far.

July 8th: Emily had a violent episode. This one was worse than anything I've seen before. She lashed out, shouting things I couldn't fully understand. For a moment, I thought she might actually attack me. I'm not sure if I can control her anymore when she's like this. I'll have to decide soon whether it's worth the risk.

The entries ended abruptly after that, as though Ian had been planning something darker, something more final. A shiver ran down Rachel's spine. Had he known that his experiments would culminate in his own death? Had he sensed that Emily's mind, fractured and forced into dark corners, would eventually snap?

This journal could expose everything. But even as she clutched the notebook, her mind racing, she knew that the real challenge was far from over. While this might sway the jury to see Emily as a victim, it also reinforced the grim reality that Emily's dissociative episodes could be dangerous.

Rachel's phone buzzed, jolting her back to the present. It was Eli.

"I found something," she said without preamble when she answered.

"Me too," Eli replied, his tone grave. "I've been going through Emily's psychiatric records again, and there are signs that Ian might have pushed her toward self-doubt deliberately. Every therapist Emily ever saw mentions her husband's influence, noting that he seemed to downplay her symptoms or outright deny her memories."

Rachel's grip on the phone tightened. "Ian wasn't just denying her symptoms—he was exacerbating them. I found his journal. He'd been manipulating her episodes, deliberately triggering her trauma."

There was a long silence on the other end before Eli spoke again, his voice barely above a whisper. "Rachel, this is huge. But you realize this also complicates things. This kind of sustained abuse could have led to... irreparable damage in her psyche."

"I know," Rachel said, her voice thick with frustration. "But this might be enough to show the jury who Emily truly is—and what Ian turned her into."

Eli sighed. "We'll have to handle this delicately. Public opinion is already hanging by a thread. They'll see her as dangerous, but maybe we can make them see her as a victim too."

Rachel closed her eyes, taking a deep breath to centre herself. "We don't have another choice. This is the best shot we've got. I'll need you to explain the implications of Ian's abuse to the jury—to make them understand the psychological impact of his actions on Emily's condition."

"Understood," Eli said. "And Rachel... be prepared. If this gets out, people may turn against us even more. But if we can get the jury to see the full picture, maybe they'll realize Emily isn't the monster they think she is."

After ending the call, Rachel sat in silence, her fingers brushing the cracked leather of the journal's cover. The document was now an essential weapon in Emily's defence—a last, desperate piece of evidence that could save her client's life. But it was also a haunting reminder of the horrors Emily had endured; of the broken mind her husband had helped create.

Rachel's resolve hardened. Tomorrow, she would lay it all out in court, bringing Ian's twisted obsession to light. She would expose his manipulation, his cruelty. She would make the world see that Emily Grant was not simply a suspect on trial, but a woman whose mind had been shattered, used as a tool for someone else's satisfaction.

As she stood and gathered her things, the weight of what lay ahead pressed down on her, yet for the first time in days, she felt a spark of hope. She had the truth in her hands, and now, it was time to set Emily free from the shadow of her husband's control.

Chapter 16: Closer to the Truth

The sterile, silent room felt tense, the air thick with the weight of what was about to unfold. Eli Warren sat across from Emily, his gaze calm yet intent as he studied her face, searching for any signs of resistance or fear. Today was a crucial step, one that could either fracture her psyche further or finally unlock the memories she'd buried so deeply.

Emily looked weary, shadows beneath her eyes and a nervous tremor in her hands as she folded them in her lap. She hadn't wanted to come today, but after seeing Rachel's determined expression after their latest court appearance, she'd felt an obligation—maybe even a spark of hope—to see this through.

"Emily," Eli began gently, his voice as calm and steady as a warm breeze, "we're going to talk about your past again, okay? Some of the things that happened to you when you were younger."

She swallowed, nodding, though her gaze remained fixed on the floor.

"I'm here with you," he assured her. "If at any point you feel overwhelmed, we can stop. But we're going to take it slow, and I want you to know that I'm right here."

The gentle rhythm of his words seemed to ease some of her tension, and she finally met his eyes. "I… I'm ready."

Eli nodded, opening his notebook and clicking his pen. "Good. I'd like you to close your eyes for a moment. Just listen to my voice and let your mind drift back. We're not looking for anything specific, just... letting memories come as they choose. Focus on the emotions, the sensations—anything that might float to the surface."

She did as instructed, breathing deeply as her eyelids fluttered shut. In the silence, he could see her posture change subtly, her shoulders loosening and her breathing slowing. After a few minutes, he began speaking again.

"Let's go back, Emily. Back to a time when you were young, back before you met Ian, before the world became as complicated as it is now. Can you remember what it felt like to be a child?"

For a moment, there was only silence. Then she whispered, "I... I used to play in the woods behind our house. There was a small clearing there, with tall grass and wildflowers. It was my secret place."

Eli smiled, making notes. "That sounds peaceful."

She nodded, her face softening. "I used to go there with my friend. Her name was Anna."

There it was—the name he'd been hoping she would say. Anna was the friend who'd died, a death that had haunted Emily's early life and had left her adrift with a deep, unacknowledged pain. Her parents had reportedly sheltered her from most of the investigation, but that choice had left scars, gaps in her memory where trauma had lived, festering and untreated.

"Tell me about Anna," Eli encouraged. "What was she like?"

"She was... brave. So much braver than me," Emily murmured. "She would climb trees and go deeper into the woods than I ever dared. She'd laugh at me for being scared of the dark, but she'd hold my hand if I got frightened."

Emily's expression softened into a wistful smile, the kind of warmth that only a treasured memory could bring. But then, her brow furrowed, her hands tightening in her lap.

"What do you remember about the last time you saw her?"

Her breathing grew shallow, and her eyes fluttered, as if resisting an unseen force. Eli reached out gently, his voice soothing.

"It's okay, Emily. Just let the memories come. Don't force anything."

Emily took a shaky breath, but as she spoke, her voice wavered, tinged with an eerie sense of detachment. "We were playing in the clearing... just the two of us. I remember... she dared me to go farther than we ever had before."

She paused, visibly trembling, her face contorted in distress. Eli leaned forward, his tone calm but insistent.

"What happened then, Emily?"

"I... I can't remember all of it." Her voice quivered. "But I remember running. The sun was setting, and I was running. She was right behind me, calling my name... but then, there was this scream, this horrible, horrible scream."

Emily's hand flew to her mouth, her expression shifting from sorrow to horror as she continued to remember. "I turned around, and she wasn't there anymore. There was just... silence."

Eli watched her carefully, reading every micro-expression, every twitch, and every flicker of her eyes. "What happened after that, Emily?"

Tears glistened in her eyes as she gripped the arms of her chair. "I went home. I didn't tell anyone what happened. I just... went home, crawled into bed, and shut my eyes. I was too afraid to say anything. I thought maybe if I just forgot about it, everything would go back to normal."

"But it didn't, did it?"

She shook her head, a hollow look in her eyes. "The police came. They asked if I'd seen her. And I said no. I lied. I was so scared, I just... lied. They searched everywhere for her, but she was gone."

Her voice cracked, and the sorrow etched into her face made her seem small and fragile, as though she were once again the child who had watched her friend vanish in the woods.

"You did what any child would do in that situation," Eli said gently, sensing her guilt. "You were scared, and you were trying to protect yourself."

But Emily was shaking her head, the tears slipping down her cheeks. "No, it was more than that. I... I felt like it was my fault. Like maybe I'd done something to her. I felt like I was the one who made her disappear."

"Why do you think that?"

Her gaze turned distant, her voice barely above a whisper. "Sometimes... sometimes I wonder if I did hurt her, even though I don't remember. I get these flashes—of her face, of the woods at dusk, and of me, standing there alone. There was so much blood."

The revelation chilled Eli, though he kept his face neutral. "Emily, do you remember hurting her? Or is it just an impression?"

"I... I don't know," she whispered, curling into herself. "Sometimes I think I do remember. Sometimes I'm sure I hurt her. And then other times, it's just... blank."

A dark realization flickered in Eli's mind. Emily's dissociative episodes weren't just moments of escape—they were reactions to overwhelming trauma, repressed memories that had never been processed, only buried deeper with each passing year.

"Emily," he said carefully, "the mind sometimes creates barriers to protect us from painful experiences. Your memories of that day may feel confusing and fragmented because your mind was trying to shield you. But that doesn't mean you're responsible."

"But it's the same," she insisted, her eyes wide with panic. "It's just like what happened with Ian. I was there, I was standing there, but I don't remember doing anything. What if… what if it's all me?"

Her voice was laced with fear, and Eli could feel the weight of her uncertainty. This was the crux of the struggle for her, the line between memory and reality, between what had been done to her and what she feared she might have done. Her childhood trauma, left untreated and festering for so long, had twisted her own memories into dark, fractured shapes.

He leaned forward, meeting her gaze with steady compassion. "Emily, your mind has been through years of pain and manipulation, not just from Ian but from the unresolved loss of Anna. Sometimes, when we experience traumatic events, our memories distort. They don't always reflect the truth. What you remember may not be what actually happened."

"But what if it is?" she whispered, fear etched in every line of her face. "What if I'm capable of… of things like that?"

Eli reached out, placing a reassuring hand over hers. "This is what we're going to figure out, together. I believe that the same fear you're feeling now shows that you are, at your core, someone who cares deeply. Someone who is capable of love and empathy."

She looked down, blinking away the tears that had gathered in her eyes. "I don't know who I am anymore. I don't know what's real."

Eli gave her hand a gentle squeeze. "You've been through more than most people could bear. But with time, and by facing these memories, you'll start to understand yourself. We're getting closer to the truth, Emily, and that truth will set you free."

Emily took a deep, shaky breath, nodding slowly. She looked back at Eli with a newfound determination, a spark of hope flickering beneath the layers of fear and doubt. For the first time, she felt as though the burden of her past might not be insurmountable.

As Eli watched her, he felt a sense of clarity. Emily wasn't a killer. She was a woman who had been shaped, broken, and manipulated by forces outside her control. The path forward would be difficult, but he was determined to help her reclaim her life—no matter the cost.

Chapter 17: The Shocking Confession

The small, dimly lit room felt stifling. Emily sat across from Eli, her eyes vacant, almost distant, as if she were somewhere else entirely. Rachel, standing by the door, watched intently. She'd seen Emily slip in and out of focus before, but there was something different about her today—a strange, unsettling calm.

"Emily," Eli began, his voice measured, careful. "We're getting closer. You've done so much hard work to bring these memories to the surface. Are you ready to talk about the night of Ian's death?"

She blinked slowly, as if awakening from a dream. But when she looked at him, her gaze was cold, devoid of the familiar softness he'd grown accustomed to.

Rachel's pulse quickened, her instincts telling her something significant was about to happen. She moved quietly to the side, her eyes never leaving Emily's face.

"I remember," Emily said, her voice low, almost a whisper. It was flat, without the tremor or hesitation that had marked her previous recollections.

"What do you remember?" Eli's tone was gentle, a lifeline in a darkening sea.

Emily's lips curled into a faint, almost mocking smile. "I remember… him."

"Who, Emily?" Rachel pressed, her voice barely above a whisper.

Emily's gaze drifted to the far wall, her expression tightening. "Ian. That night… he was in my way."

The words came out strange, unnatural. Eli exchanged a quick glance with Rachel, signalling caution. He leaned forward, his posture open and inviting, though his mind was racing.

"Can you tell us more?" he asked softly.

Emily's eyes narrowed. "He thought he could control me; thought he could make me… small. Weak." Her voice was bitter, laced with an anger that neither Eli nor Rachel had heard from her before.

The room grew colder as Emily continued, her voice dropping to a menacing murmur. "But I was stronger than he thought. I was ready. And when he pushed me, I… I fought back."

Rachel's throat tightened, a wave of dread washing over her. Emily's tone, her words—it was as if they were coming from someone else entirely. Her voice was sharper, darker. This wasn't the Emily she knew.

"Emily," Eli spoke slowly, carefully. "Who are you right now?"

She tilted her head, her gaze shifting back to him. "Who am I?" she echoed, her lips curving into a sinister smile. "I am what he made me. I am the one who protects her."

Eli felt a chill creep down his spine. He had suspected the presence of alternate identities within Emily's psyche, fragments created as defence mechanisms against trauma, but he hadn't encountered one this… assertive.

"What's your name?" he asked carefully, his voice as calm as possible.

The woman who was Emily smirked, leaning back in her chair. "Names don't matter. I'm the one who does what Emily can't. The one who took care of things when Ian got too close."

A tense silence filled the room. Rachel looked to Eli, her expression full of questions and an unspoken plea for guidance.

"Why did you do it?" Eli asked, leaning forward.

She raised an eyebrow, as if the question amused her. "He was hurting her. He thought he could keep pushing her, breaking her down until there was nothing left. But he didn't know she wasn't alone. He didn't know I was there."

Rachel's hands clenched by her sides. She was witnessing something extraordinary, but it was terrifying, too. This wasn't a simple confession. It was a confession from a part of Emily that was both her and somehow… not her.

"Can you tell us what happened that night?" Eli's tone was steady, his gaze unwavering.

She seemed to consider the question, her eyes shifting as if replaying the events in her mind. "He was waiting for her. Watching her with that smug look he always had, as if he owned her. She felt it, the way he got under her skin, crawled into her mind. But he didn't see me coming."

A flicker of pain crossed her face, but it was quickly replaced by a hard, steely resolve. "I made sure he couldn't hurt her anymore."

Rachel felt her chest tighten, her mind reeling. This wasn't a straightforward confession—it was a window into the fractured depths of Emily's mind, where memories and personas twisted together, creating an alternate self-born out of survival.

"So, you… protected her?" Eli's voice was cautious, gentle.

She nodded slowly. "Yes. And she doesn't remember. She can't remember, because I did it for her."

The weight of her words hung in the air, and Rachel's pulse quickened. She knew what this meant—if the court heard this, it could reshape the entire case. But it was dangerous, too. It walked the fine line between insanity and culpability, between Emily's innocence and guilt.

Eli took a breath, studying her intently. "Emily, I want to speak to you now. Can you come back?"

For a moment, she was silent. Then her expression softened, her eyes losing that cold edge as she blinked, disoriented. "Eli?" she murmured, confusion clouding her face.

"Yes, Emily. I'm here."

She looked around, frowning. "I... I don't remember what happened. Did I say something?"

Eli exchanged a look with Rachel, nodding slowly. "You did. We talked about that night. You remembered something."

A flicker of fear crossed her face, and she shook her head. "No... I don't... I don't remember anything."

"Emily," Rachel spoke gently, stepping closer. "Do you remember someone protecting you? Someone stepping in when you couldn't?"

Her eyes darted between them, fear and confusion intertwining. "I... sometimes I feel like there's someone else. Someone stronger. Someone who doesn't let anyone hurt me."

A tear slipped down her cheek, and she looked away, her voice breaking. "But that night... I don't know. I don't know what's real."

Rachel placed a reassuring hand on her shoulder. "Emily, what you just shared with us—it might be a part of you that's trying to protect you. And that's okay. You're not alone in this."

Emily took a shaky breath, her gaze haunted. "I'm so scared, Rachel. I don't know who I am anymore. I feel like a stranger in my own body."

Eli leaned forward, his voice soothing. "Emily, this is part of your journey. Understanding these parts of yourself is the first step toward healing. You've been through so much, and your mind has found ways to help you survive. But now it's time to confront those memories, to face them so they don't control you anymore."

She nodded, though her expression was still uncertain, lost. "I just... I want to know the truth. But I don't know if I can handle it."

"We'll take this one step at a time," Eli assured her. "You're not facing this alone."

As the session came to a close, Rachel and Eli exchanged a glance that held a mix of hope and trepidation. They were closer to the truth than ever, but they were also walking a tightrope between Emily's fragile mental state and the harsh reality of the law. If this other persona, this "protector," had indeed surfaced that night, then proving her innocence would become more complex and precarious.

The confession they'd just heard blurred the boundaries between Emily's trauma and her actions. It was an admission, but from a fragmented mind—a mind that had fractured to survive. Rachel felt the weight of their task pressing down on her, the ethical and emotional gravity of defending a client who was both a victim and a potential perpetrator in the eyes of the law.

As they left the room, Eli pulled Rachel aside, his face pale but resolute. "This changes everything, Rachel. We're dealing with something far more complex than I initially thought."

She nodded, her expression solemn. "I know. But this—this is the truth we've been searching for. And now that we're here, we can't turn back. We have to find a way to make the court see Emily for who she truly is, even if she doesn't know it herself."

Eli looked at her, determination and trepidation swirling in his gaze. "Then we move forward. Whatever it takes."

They left the building together, both aware that the real battle had only just begun. The truth they'd uncovered was powerful, but it was also fragile, balanced precariously between Emily's fractured psyche and the unforgiving scrutiny of the courtroom. As they walked into the night, Rachel knew one thing for certain: the stakes had never been higher, and failure was not an option.

Chapter 18: The Final Argument

The courtroom felt heavier than ever, its silence dense and charged with the weight of everything that had been said, uncovered, and exposed. This was the last day, the day that would determine everything. Rachel stood before the jury, her heart pounding as she scanned their faces. She had to find a way to reach them, to make them see Emily not as a monster, but as a woman cornered by life, by trauma, and by those who claimed to love her.

Rachel took a deep breath, focusing on her notes for just a moment before letting them fall to the table. This was not the time for rehearsed lines or legal jargon; this was the time to speak from the heart.

"Ladies and gentlemen of the jury," she began, her voice steady but laced with the slightest tremor of emotion. "What we're here to decide today is not just a question of guilt or innocence. We're here to look at the complexity of a life and to understand how trauma can twist our very sense of reality, leaving scars that are invisible to the eye but deeply etched into the soul."

Rachel paused, letting her words sink in, feeling the jury's gaze settle on her as she continued.

"We've heard so much over these past weeks. We've dissected the life of a woman who is, in many ways, more a survivor than anything else. Emily Grant has endured unimaginable hardships, and while I know the details may have made some of us uncomfortable, it is essential to acknowledge them. Because they're at the core of why we're here. Trauma, manipulation, and abuse are not excuses. They are explanations—explanations for the unthinkable ways people are forced to adapt to survive."

She paced slightly, stopping near the jury box, her gaze steady, her voice lowering. "Let me ask you to imagine something: Imagine you're a child, growing up in a home where the very people who are meant to protect you become a source of terror. You learn to fragment yourself, to hide parts of who you are just to survive. Imagine carrying that into adulthood, where you find yourself controlled, manipulated, used by someone who should have loved you. What would that do to your mind? To your sense of reality?"

Rachel paused, giving them a moment to let the hypothetical settle. She knew she couldn't erase the image of Emily standing over Ian's body, the blood that seemed to cry out for justice. But she could at least offer a path to understanding.

"Emily didn't kill her husband out of malice, or hate, or cruelty. She did it because her mind, fractured and broken by years of trauma, failed her in that moment. She wasn't herself. The Emily who loved Ian, the Emily who would never have wanted harm to come to him, she was pushed aside by something created from years of pain and survival instincts. Something that was beyond her control."

Rachel's gaze softened as she looked at the jury, her expression earnest. "We are not here to excuse her actions, but we are here to understand them. This case is about recognizing the limits of the human mind under relentless stress, about acknowledging that sometimes, people are not fully responsible for the things they do when they are living in a reality shaped by trauma and fear."

A murmur passed through the gallery, the impact of her words resonating in the tension that filled the room. Rachel sensed the shift, the ripple of empathy that she was so desperately hoping to evoke. But it was fragile, easily shaken by the prosecutor's looming rebuttal.

Rachel turned to face the judge, her final words resonating. "I ask you to see Emily Grant not as a cold-blooded killer, but as a woman who has been fighting her whole life—against forces beyond her control, within and without. She deserves understanding, not condemnation. For this one tragic act was not her alone; it was the culmination of a life marked by suffering. It was the result of wounds that ran so deep they fractured her very sense of self."

She took a breath, letting the weight of her words settle. "You, ladies and gentlemen of the jury, have the power to offer her compassion, the compassion she's never known. That's all I ask. Thank you."

Rachel returned to her seat, her hands trembling slightly as she sat. Eli, seated beside her, gave her a supportive nod, his face a mixture of pride and worry. She'd done everything she could, laid Emily's pain and history bare for all to see. Now, it was up to the jury.

The judge called a brief recess before the prosecution's closing statement. Rachel barely heard the announcement, her mind swirling with worry. She glanced at Emily, who looked both hopeful and afraid. It was a fragile hope, but it was all they had.

When the prosecutor stood, the courtroom felt colder, as if the temperature had dropped a few degrees. The man's expression was stern, his gaze sharp as he began his rebuttal.

"Ladies and gentlemen of the jury," he started, his voice cutting through the air like a knife. "What you've just heard is a tragic story, no doubt about it. But we're not here to decide whether Emily Grant's life was difficult. We're here to determine if she took a life in cold blood."

He walked to the jury, looking each of them in the eye as he continued, "Let's not lose sight of what's at stake. A man, Ian Grant, is dead. And as tragic as her history may be, as much as we may sympathize with the challenges Emily faced, we cannot ignore the facts. Emily Grant was found standing over her husband's body, covered in his blood, holding the very weapon that killed him."

He turned, his voice rising slightly. "Ms. Yates has argued that Emily's mind was 'fractured,' that her trauma created this... this alter who committed the act. But let's take a step back. How convenient is it that her mental illness only manifests in these moments of violence? What about the moments when she led a normal life, when she managed to function without any evidence of this so-called 'other self'? Mental illness is real, and it is tragic, but it does not absolve one of murder."

Rachel felt a pit forming in her stomach. The prosecutor was ruthless, driving his point home with unyielding force.

"Let's also consider this: Emily Grant never sought help, never took steps to address her mental health despite having ample resources. Instead, she allowed herself to live with this 'dangerous alter' lurking within her, making her a threat not only to her husband but to society."

He paused, allowing his words to settle, letting the jury feel the weight of his argument. "If we start excusing every act of violence based on a tragic past or an alleged mental illness, where do we draw the line? How many more victims must suffer because we fail to hold people accountable? Emily Grant's actions were deliberate, and there is no evidence—no clear proof—that she was incapable of understanding her actions. She should be held responsible."

The prosecutor took a breath, his gaze intense. "Ladies and gentlemen, you have a duty to uphold justice. Justice for Ian Grant, who can no longer speak for himself. The defence would have you pity his killer, would have you believe she was just a puppet of her own mind, but that doesn't change the outcome. Ian Grant is dead, and his killer is sitting right there."

He pointed at Emily, who shrank under the attention, visibly trembling. The jury's eyes were on her, many of them hard, unforgiving. Rachel's heart sank. The prosecutor had struck at their emotions, redirecting sympathy from Emily back to Ian, making it impossible to ignore the life that had been lost.

He finished with a final, cutting line. "Justice isn't about pity. It's about accountability. And it's about making sure that people who commit heinous acts face the consequences. I urge you to remember that, for Ian's sake. Thank you."

The courtroom fell silent as the prosecutor returned to his seat; his expression grimly satisfied. Rachel felt a knot of dread coil in her stomach, the force of his words echoing in her mind.

She looked at Emily, who was pale, trembling, the weight of the prosecutor's words clearly pressing down on her. Rachel reached over, offering her hand, and Emily gripped it tightly, her knuckles white.

Rachel had done everything she could. She'd painted a picture of a woman broken, struggling, a woman who had suffered beyond measure. But in the eyes of the jury, it was unclear if that would be enough. The prosecutor's words hung heavily, and the gravity of the decision lay in the hands of the twelve strangers before them.

The judge dismissed the court, leaving the room steeped in a tense silence. Rachel walked out with Eli and Emily, each step feeling heavier than the last. The next time they'd all be back here; they'd know Emily's fate. And as much as she'd hoped for the best, Rachel couldn't shake the haunting fear that their case, built on compassion and understanding, might not be enough against a world demanding retribution.

Chapter 19: Verdict and Aftermath

The courtroom was silent as the jury filed back into their seats, their faces unreadable, their eyes steely and focused. The judge, seated at his elevated bench, waited patiently as the foreman stood, holding the small slip of paper that would define Emily's fate. Rachel could feel the heat of her own breath, the air too thin, the tension so thick it felt like it might suffocate her. Eli sat beside her, his expression grim and unreadable, his fingers tapping nervously against the wood of the table.

"Will the jury foreman please rise?" the judge's voice cut through the air like a gavel strike, heavy and final.

The foreman stood, his posture stiff, his gaze flitting across the room. He held the slip of paper high, his hand trembling slightly, betraying the weight of the decision he had just participated in.

Rachel's heart pounded, and she fought to keep her composure. She had spent the last few weeks building a case she believed in, one that painted Emily as a victim, as someone who had been broken by life and circumstance, not a cold-blooded killer. But now, standing on the precipice of everything she had worked for, she wasn't sure if it would be enough. She wasn't sure if the jury could see Emily the way she did—fragile, fractured, but ultimately human.

The foreman cleared his throat, looking first at the judge, then down at the paper in his hands.

"We, the jury, find the defendant, Emily Grant, guilty of manslaughter in the second degree."

Rachel's stomach dropped. The words seemed to reverberate through her mind in a distorted echo, unrecognizable at first. *Guilty... Manslaughter...* Her thoughts scrambled, trying to piece together the significance of those words.

Manslaughter. Not murder. Not first-degree. But not innocence either.

A pang of relief washed over her, though it was quickly replaced by a cold weight pressing against her chest. She had fought for Emily's freedom. She had fought for her to be seen as a victim of trauma, of manipulation, of a mind that had fractured under unbearable pressure. But this verdict—this middle ground—felt like a betrayal of everything they had argued for. It felt like a compromise that didn't fully acknowledge the depth of Emily's suffering. Yet, it wasn't an outright condemnation either.

The room felt suffocating as the judge motioned for the bailiff to approach.

"Thank you, jury. You are dismissed," the judge said, his voice devoid of emotion.

The foreman sat down, and the rest of the jury shuffled, their faces a blur of conflicting emotions. Some appeared exhausted, others were steely-eyed, and a few even avoided eye contact with Emily, clearly uncomfortable with the decision they had just rendered.

Rachel leaned forward; her breath tight in her chest. She tried to meet Emily's gaze, but Emily was looking down, her hands clasped tightly in her lap, her face unreadable. It was as though Emily had already retreated into herself, too afraid to face the consequences of what had just been decided.

The bailiff called for order, and the judge began speaking again, his tone impassive as he read the sentence.

"The court will reconvene in one week for sentencing," he said, his voice echoing in the otherwise quiet room. "Until then, the defendant is remanded into custody."

At that moment, Emily's composure cracked. A single sob broke the silence, followed by a desperate, strangled cry as she buried her face in her hands. Rachel rushed to her side, her heart breaking for the woman who had become both a client and someone she had grown to care for deeply.

Emily's body shook with the force of her tears, her sobs loud and raw, each one carrying the weight of everything she had tried to hold inside. The courtroom was a blur around Rachel as she knelt beside Emily, trying to offer some comfort, though it seemed so insignificant in the face of the storm Emily was enduring.

"I—I didn't mean to," Emily whispered through her tears, her voice barely audible. "I didn't mean to hurt him. I don't remember... I don't remember."

Rachel's heart clenched. She knew this wasn't just about the verdict. It wasn't just about the law. Emily was lost in a labyrinth of memories she couldn't fully access, a mind trapped between realities—victim and perpetrator, survivor and killer.

Rachel gently placed a hand on Emily's back, offering whatever solace she could. "It's okay, Emily. You're not alone. We'll figure this out. We'll get you the help you need."

Eli stood behind them, his face etched with concern, but he said nothing. The weight of the verdict seemed to weigh equally on both of them. It wasn't the victory Rachel had hoped for. It wasn't the redemption she had fought for. But there was still hope. There was still a chance for Emily to heal, to be treated, to finally face the consequences of her actions without losing herself in the process.

Later, in the sterile, quiet corridor outside the courtroom, Rachel stood with Eli, both of them staring at the door where Emily had been led away by the guards. The weight of the decision hung in the air, suffocating in its own right. They had fought with everything they had, and yet, the outcome felt so... so incomplete.

"Do you think it's enough?" Eli asked quietly, his voice tinged with doubt.

Rachel took a deep breath, her eyes focused on the ground. She wasn't sure. In a way, it felt like a failure—like they hadn't managed to break through the walls Emily had built around herself. They hadn't been able to unravel the depths of her trauma in the way they had hoped. And yet, manslaughter was not the same as murder. The jury had found her guilty, but they had acknowledged that there was more to the story.

"I don't know," Rachel admitted, her voice cracking slightly. "It feels like a compromise. We fought so hard to show them that Emily wasn't just a killer, that she wasn't just a monster. But they didn't see her as a victim, not fully. And they didn't see her as innocent either."

Eli nodded; his expression unreadable. "It's the best we could have hoped for. The best Emily could have hoped for. But sometimes, Rachel... sometimes justice isn't black and white. It's shades of grey, and that's what we've got here. It's not perfect, but it's something."

She turned to him, the weight of their shared experience settling between them like an unspoken truth. "I just wish she could see it that way. I wish she could understand that this isn't the end for her. There's still a chance for her to rebuild, to heal."

Rachel's mind drifted to the moment when Emily had broken down in court, when the rawness of her fear and pain had become impossible to ignore. She wasn't just a woman on trial for murder—she was a woman who had been pushed to the edge by a lifetime of suffering. She wasn't a monster. She was just... broken.

"I'll do everything I can," Rachel whispered, more to herself than to Eli. "I'll make sure she gets the treatment she needs. She's not beyond help."

Eli gave her a sad smile. "I know you will. We'll both make sure of it."

As the day drew to a close, and the courtroom emptied out, Rachel couldn't shake the feeling that their work wasn't done. The case might be over, but Emily's journey—her struggle for understanding, for healing, for redemption—was just beginning.

And for the first time in a long time, Rachel allowed herself to believe that, somehow, there was still hope for her.

Chapter 20: Reflections and Shadows

The sun was beginning its descent as Rachel walked down the sterile, dimly lit corridor of the correctional facility, her footsteps echoing in the silence. The walls felt cold, their pale, unforgiving concrete a reminder of the finality of Emily's new reality. The case was over. The trial, the verdict—it was all behind them now. But the lingering weight of the past few weeks hung heavily in the air, pressing against her chest with each step she took.

Eli had left her an hour ago, retreating to the safety of his office where he could process the events of the trial in his own way. Rachel understood. He had been a steady presence throughout this tumultuous journey, but even he had limits. She didn't blame him for stepping away; he had given everything he could. And now, it was time for her to face Emily alone.

She reached the visitation room, the glass partition between them still as cold and impassive as the walls outside. The guard behind the counter acknowledged her with a brief nod, unlocking the door. Rachel didn't need to say anything. There was no need for words to explain why she was here—she had to see Emily. She had to see the woman she had fought so hard to defend.

Inside the room, Emily sat at a table, her head down, her hands clasped tightly together. She looked smaller than Rachel remembered, more fragile somehow, as though the weight of the world had pressed her down into something unrecognizable. The woman who had sat on the witness stand was gone, replaced by someone more raw, more broken.

Emily's eyes flickered up as Rachel sat down across from her, and for a moment, neither of them spoke.

"Hey," Rachel finally said, her voice quieter than she intended. "How are you?"

Emily's lips quivered, but she didn't answer. She simply met Rachel's gaze, as though the question itself was too heavy to bear. Her face was gaunt, her skin pale, her eyes hollow. She looked as if the world had chewed her up and spit her out, leaving her to grapple with pieces of a shattered identity.

Rachel watched her for a long moment, waiting for Emily to find the words. She had always been patient with her clients, but today, patience felt like an almost unbearable burden. The guilt, the fear, the shame that Emily had carried for so long had finally been acknowledged in the eyes of the law. But the pain wasn't over. Rachel knew that. No verdict, no ruling could erase the scars Emily had left on her soul.

"I don't know what I'm supposed to do now," Emily whispered, her voice cracking, and Rachel's heart twisted at the sound.

"You don't have to have all the answers right now," Rachel said softly. "We're going to make sure you get the help you need. It's not over for you, Emily. You have a chance to heal. You have a chance to move forward."

Emily's eyes filled with tears, but she didn't cry. She simply stared at the table in front of her, her hands twisting in knots, her mind clearly miles away. Rachel leaned forward, her voice low and steady.

"You've been through so much, Emily. More than anyone should ever have to bear. But you're not alone in this. We'll make sure of that."

"I don't know who I am anymore," Emily whispered, her voice trembling with the admission. "I don't know if I was a victim or if I'm just… just guilty. Sometimes it feels like I don't even know what's real."

Rachel's throat tightened, the words she had prepared seeming so small and insignificant in the face of Emily's anguish. What could she say? What could she offer that could truly heal the deep wounds that had shaped Emily's life?

"You're both," Rachel said finally, her voice thick with emotion. "You're both. You were a victim of something that was beyond your control. And you're not guilty. You didn't deserve what happened to you. But that doesn't mean that what happened with your husband was any less real. The things you did, Emily… those are real, too."

The silence stretched between them, thick and suffocating, as Emily absorbed the weight of Rachel's words. There was no easy answer, no neat resolution to the complex, messy truth that Rachel had fought to uncover. The line between victim and perpetrator was always more blurred than anyone cared to admit. Emily was both—a product of abuse, manipulation, and a mind that had fractured under the pressure of it all.

"I don't know if I can forgive myself," Emily whispered, her voice barely audible, as though the very act of speaking the words felt like an unbearable burden.

"Maybe you don't need to forgive yourself yet," Rachel said softly, leaning forward. "Maybe you just need to learn to live with yourself first. To understand who you are, who you've always been. Healing is a journey. And it's not a straight line."

Emily's eyes flickered, a brief spark of something like hope flashing across her face. But it was fleeting, quickly buried beneath the weight of her doubt.

"But what about the people I hurt?" Emily's voice was barely a whisper. "What about… what about him?"

Rachel hesitated, the question of Emily's husband hanging in the air like an unspoken ghost. He was dead. There was no bringing him back, no undoing the damage done. But Emily's responsibility in his death—whether as a victim or as a participant—would linger, unanswered, forever.

"The people you hurt… they'll never forget," Rachel said, her voice quiet but firm. "But you can't keep carrying that weight forever. At some point, you have to let go of the guilt. You have to let yourself move forward."

Emily's face crumpled, and this time, the tears came—slow at first, then faster, until they were streaming down her face, each tear a painful release of the emotions she had kept hidden for so long.

"I don't know if I can," she sobbed. "I don't know if I can ever escape this."

Rachel reached across the table, placing a hand on Emily's trembling one. The contact felt like the first step toward something—perhaps not healing, but understanding. Not forgiveness, but a recognition of the complexity of the human heart. Sometimes, there were no easy answers, no perfect solutions. Sometimes, the only thing a person could do was survive.

"You will," Rachel said softly, her voice resolute despite the uncertainty swirling in her own heart. "You'll find a way."

Later, as Rachel stepped out of the visitation room, her mind was a whirlwind of conflicting thoughts. She had seen Emily—really seen her—in a way that no one else had. Not as a case, not as a client, but as a woman who had suffered beyond measure. Rachel knew she had done her best. She had fought for Emily when no one else would, and now, the battle was no longer hers to fight.

But there was still a question that lingered, unanswered in her mind. A question that had been gnawing at her since the trial had begun: *What does it mean to defend someone like Emily?*

Society wanted answers, wanted a clear-cut distinction between right and wrong, good and bad. But Rachel knew better. She had seen the shades of grey, the murky waters between innocence and guilt. She had fought to expose the truth, but she knew that truth was never as simple as a courtroom verdict. It was complicated, messy, and layered with things that no one cared to see.

In the end, that was what this case had taught her—the line between victim and perpetrator was a fine one, and sometimes, the people society condemned the most were the ones who needed saving the most.

Rachel paused in the hallway, staring out through the small window at the grey sky. The weight of the case, the weight of Emily's pain, was still pressing down on her. She didn't know if Emily would ever find peace. But Rachel had to hope. Because hope, even in the darkest of times, was the only thing that could carry them both forward.

And as she walked out of the prison, leaving the past behind her, Rachel couldn't help but wonder: *If everyone deserves a second chance, who decides if they get it?*

Appendices

Appendix A: Understanding Dissociative Identity Disorder (DID)

Dissociative Identity Disorder (DID), formerly known as Multiple Personality Disorder, is a complex psychological condition characterized by the presence of two or more distinct identity states within a single individual. These identities may have their own unique behaviours, memories, and ways of perceiving the world. DID often results from severe trauma, particularly in early childhood, and serves as a coping mechanism, allowing individuals to dissociate from painful experiences. This novel touches on DID as part of its exploration of trauma and mental health in the legal system, acknowledging both the controversies and the ongoing research surrounding the condition.

Appendix B: Legal Definitions and Concepts

1. **Insanity Defence**
   In legal terms, the insanity defence argues that the defendant was not in a state to comprehend the nature of their actions or distinguish between right and wrong due to a severe mental disorder at the time of the crime. Each legal system has specific criteria for establishing insanity, and cases involving mental illness require complex evidence from mental health professionals.

2. **Diminished Capacity**
   This concept refers to situations where a defendant may not meet the full criteria for insanity but, due to a mental disorder, lacked the intent required to commit certain types of crimes. It does not

absolve them of responsibility but may reduce the severity of charges or punishment.

3. **The Burden of Proof**
In criminal cases, the burden of proof rests on the prosecution, requiring them to prove the defendant's guilt "beyond a reasonable doubt." However, in cases involving mental health defences, both the defence and prosecution may need to present substantial evidence on the defendant's mental state.

Appendix C: The Psychological and Legal Implications of Trauma

Trauma is a profound psychological impact that can alter behaviour, cognition, and emotional responses. Many individuals with DID have histories of severe trauma, often leading to coping mechanisms that challenge traditional legal accountability. The novel examines how trauma can complicate the pursuit of justice, particularly when trauma itself becomes a potential factor in the behaviour being prosecuted.
This appendix serves as a reminder of the importance of empathy and understanding in both psychological assessment and legal proceedings.

Appendix D: Additional Resources

For readers interested in learning more about the topics covered in *The Mind's Verdict*, here are a few recommended books and resources:

1. **Books on Dissociative Identity Disorder (DID):**

    - *The Stranger in the Mirror: Dissociation—The Hidden Epidemic* by Marlene Steinberg and Maxine Schnall
    - *Switching Time: A Doctor's Harrowing Story of Treating a Woman with 17 Personalities* by Richard Baer

2. **Books on the Legal System and Mental Health:**

- *Insanity: Murder, Madness, and the Law* by Charles Patrick Ewing
- *The Myth of Mental Illness: Foundations of a Theory of Personal Conduct* by Thomas Szasz

3. **Online Resources:**
    - The American Psychological Association (APA) website: www.apa.org
    - National Alliance on Mental Illness (NAMI): www.nami.org

Glossary

A

- **Alter Persona**
  A distinct identity or personality state within a person with dissociative identity disorder (DID). Each alter may have its own unique name, history, and traits, serving different roles in managing trauma.

- **Amnesia**
  A partial or total loss of memory, often related to trauma or psychological disorders. In cases of DID, individuals may experience memory gaps due to dissociative episodes.

B

- **Burden of Proof**
  The obligation of a party in a legal proceeding, typically the prosecution, to prove their allegations with sufficient evidence. In criminal cases, this is met when the evidence establishes guilt "beyond a reasonable doubt."

D

- **Dissociation**
  A psychological condition where an individual feels detached from reality or their sense of self, often as a response to trauma.

This can include memory gaps, altered perceptions, and identity shifts.

- **Dissociative Identity Disorder (DID)**
  A mental health condition characterized by the presence of two or more distinct identity states. DID typically develops as a coping mechanism in response to severe trauma, particularly in early childhood.

- **Diminished Capacity**
  A legal concept that recognizes a defendant may lack full mental capacity, which can affect intent or responsibility in criminal cases. It does not exonerate the defendant but can lead to lesser charges or sentences.

E

- **Expert Witness**
  A professional, such as a psychologist or forensic specialist, who provides specialized knowledge and opinions in court. Their insights help the jury and judge understand complex issues related to the case.

H

- **Hypnosis**
  A therapeutic technique that places individuals in a focused state of relaxation, often used to recover repressed memories or explore the subconscious mind. It is controversial as a reliable method in legal cases.

I

- **Insanity Defence**
  A legal argument asserting that a defendant was unable to comprehend the nature of their actions or distinguish right from wrong due to mental illness. Successful pleas of insanity may lead to treatment instead of prison.

J

- **Jury**
  A group of citizens selected to examine the evidence and determine the outcome in a trial. Jurors are charged with delivering an impartial verdict based on the facts presented in court.

M

- **Manipulation**
  In psychology and law, this refers to the influence or control exerted by one person over another's actions or beliefs, often through deceit or exploitation. It can play a significant role in cases involving abuse and coercion.

- **Mental Health Evaluation**
  An assessment conducted by a licensed mental health professional to diagnose and understand a person's psychological state, often used in court to determine competency or mental illness.

N

- **Not Guilty by Reason of Insanity (NGRI)**
  A verdict acknowledging that the defendant committed the act but was legally insane at the time. This leads to treatment rather

than incarceration, though the defendant may still face restrictions.

P

- **Post-Traumatic Stress Disorder (PTSD)**
  A mental health condition triggered by experiencing or witnessing a traumatic event. Symptoms may include flashbacks, severe anxiety, and uncontrollable thoughts related to the trauma.

- **Prosecutor**
  A legal representative of the state responsible for presenting the case against a defendant in a criminal trial. The prosecutor seeks to prove the defendant's guilt based on the evidence.

R

- **Repressed Memory**
  A memory of a traumatic event that has been unconsciously blocked from conscious recall. It can resurface through therapy or triggers and is sometimes controversial in court due to concerns about reliability.

T

- **Trauma**
  A deeply distressing or disturbing experience that can have lasting psychological effects. Trauma is often a central element in cases involving mental health defences.

- **Trial**
  The formal examination of evidence in a court to determine a defendant's guilt or innocence. The trial process includes jury

selection, opening statements, witness testimonies, and closing arguments.

V

- **Verdict**
  The decision made by a jury or judge regarding the guilt or innocence of the defendant. It concludes the trial, though appeals or sentencing may follow

Bibliography

In preparing *The Mind's Verdict*, I consulted various sources to ensure accuracy in representing legal procedures, psychological conditions, and forensic practices. Below is a list of resources that were invaluable in crafting this story and providing insights into dissociative identity disorder, the insanity defence, and the broader intersection of mental health and criminal law.

Books

- American Psychiatric Association. *Diagnostic and Statistical Manual of Mental Disorders (DSM-5)*. American Psychiatric Publishing, 2013.
    - A critical resource for understanding mental health diagnoses, including dissociative identity disorder, and the symptoms associated with dissociative and traumatic conditions.
- Kaplan, Harold I., and Benjamin J. Sadock. *Comprehensive Textbook of Psychiatry*. Lippincott Williams & Wilkins, 2005.
    - An in-depth guide on psychiatric disorders, covering the psychological theories and clinical practices relevant to trauma and dissociation.
- Loftus, Elizabeth F., and Katherine Ketcham. *The Myth of Repressed Memory: False Memories and Allegations of Sexual Abuse*. St. Martin's Press, 1994.

- o   A critical examination of memory reliability, repressed memories, and the ethical concerns that arise in legal settings.

- Saks, Elyn R. *The Centre Cannot Hold: My Journey Through Madness.* Hyperion, 2007.

  - o   An autobiographical account providing insight into mental illness from a legal scholar's perspective, bridging the personal and legal aspects of mental health issues.

- Simon, Robert I., and Daniel W. Shuman. *Clinical Manual of Psychiatry and Law.* American Psychiatric Publishing, 2007.

  - o   Offers a comprehensive overview of psychiatry's role within the legal system, addressing issues like competence, criminal responsibility, and expert witness testimony.

Articles

- Borum, Randy, et al. "Psychological Evaluations for the Courts: A Handbook for Mental Health Professionals and Lawyers." *American Academy of Psychiatry and the Law Journal*, vol. 23, no. 2, 1995, pp. 121–138.

  - o   A foundational article on psychological evaluations in the courtroom, crucial for understanding the role of forensic psychology in legal cases.

- Melton, Gary B., et al. "Mental Health Assessments in the Criminal Justice System." *American Psychologist*, vol. 53, no. 6, 1998, pp. 622–632.

  - o   Explores the ethical implications and methodologies of mental health assessments used to determine criminal responsibility.

Case Law and Legal References

- U.S. Supreme Court. *Ford v. Wainwright*, 477 U.S. 399 (1986).
    - A landmark case examining the constitutional limits of criminal responsibility and mental health, which informed aspects of the insanity defence presented in *The Mind's Verdict*.
- **Legal Encyclopaedia and Texts on Criminal Law**
  Standard legal reference works were consulted to accurately depict trial procedures, rules of evidence, and the burden of proof required in criminal cases.

Additional Resources

- **National Institute of Mental Health (NIMH).**
  Provides up-to-date research and statistical data on mental health disorders, contributing to the accurate portrayal of dissociative and other mental health conditions in the novel.

- **American Psychological Association (APA).**
  Consulted for guidelines on ethics and practice standards for psychologists in forensic settings, informing Eli's role as an expert witness.

Author Biography

Jerome Wright is an emerging novelist and storyteller, known for weaving intricate psychological and legal thrillers that explore the moral complexities of the human mind. With an interest in law and a deep interest in psychology, Jerome brings authenticity and insight to his writing, crafting narratives that resonate with readers who are drawn to stories of justice, mental health, and ethical dilemmas.

Born and raised in Ocho Rios, Jamaica, Jerome has a unique perspective that informs his storytelling. He has published multiple novels across genres, including thrillers, mysteries, and contemporary romance. Among his notable works are *Tropical Romance*, a heartwarming tale of love set against the vibrant backdrop of Jamaica, and *Shadows on the Painted Street*, a psychological thriller set in London that follows a detective's pursuit of a killer with a chilling obsession.

The Mind's Verdict is the first book in Jerome's *Minds of Justice* series, delving into the intersection of law and psychology as it questions the boundaries of guilt and innocence. Through his work, Jerome aims to captivate readers while provoking thought on the complex nature of truth, memory, and moral responsibility.

When he isn't writing, Jerome enjoys exploring abandoned cities for inspiration, as seen in his upcoming nonfiction work, *Invisible Cities: A Journey Through Abandoned Towns*. He is passionate about bringing to life stories that challenge perceptions and explore the hidden parts of the human experience.